The Dragon with a Chocolate Heart

The Dragon with a Chocolate Heart

STEPHANIE BURGIS

BLOOMSBURY

LONDON OXFORD NEW YORK NEW DELHI SYDNEY

Bloomsbury Publishing, London, Oxford, New York, New Delhi and Sydney

First published in Great Britain in February 2017 by Bloomsbury Publishing Plc
50 Bedford Square, London WC1B 3DP

www.bloomsbury.com

A CIP catalogue record for this book is available from the British Library

ISBN 978 1 4088 8031 9

Typeset by RefineCatch Limited, Bungay, Suffolk
Printed and bound in Great Britain by CPI Group (UK) Ltd, Croydon CR0 4YY

1 3 5 7 9 10 8 6 4 2

For Jamie Samphire.
I love you even more than chocolate!

CHAPTER 1

I can't say I ever wondered what it felt like to be human. But then, my grandfather Grenat always said, 'It's *safer not to talk to your food*,' – and as every dragon knows, humans are the most dangerous kind of meal there is.

Of course, as a young dragon, all I ever saw of them were their jewels and their books. The jewels were delightful, but their books were just maddening. What a waste of ink! No matter how hard I squinted, I could never make it past the first few paragraphs of cramped, crabby text. The last time I tried, I got so frustrated I burned three of those books to cinders with angry puffs of my breath.

'Don't you have any higher feelings?' my brother demanded, when he saw what I'd done. Jasper wanted to be a philosopher, so he always tried to stay calm, but his tail began to lash dangerously, sending gold coins showering through our cavern as he glared at the smoking pile before me. 'Just think,' he told me. 'Every one of those books was written by a creature whose brain was half the size of one of your forefeet. And yet, apparently, even *they* have more patience than you!'

'Oh, really?' I loved goading high-minded Jasper into losing his temper ... and now that I'd laid waste to my tiny paper enemies, I was ready for fun. So I braced myself, scales rippling with secret delight, and said, 'Well, I think anyone who wants to spend his time reading ant scribbles must have an ant-sized brain himself.'

'Arrrrgh!'

He let out the most satisfying roar of rage and leaped forward, landing exactly where I'd been sitting only a moment ago. If I hadn't been expecting it, I would have been slammed into a mountain of loose diamonds and emeralds, and my still-soft scales would have been bruised all over. But Jasper was the one who landed there instead, while I joyously pounced on his back and rubbed his snout in the pile of rocks.

'Children!' Our mother raised her head from her forefeet and let out a long-suffering snort that blew through the cave, sending more gold coins flying. 'Some of us are trying to sleep after a long, hard hunt!'

'I would have helped you hunt,' I said, jumping off Jasper. 'If you'd let me come –'

'Your scales haven't hardened enough to withstand even a wolf's bite.' Mother's great head sank back down towards her glittering blue-and-gold feet. 'Let alone a bullet or a mage's spell,' she added wearily. 'In another thirty years, perhaps, when you're nearly grown and ready to fly ...'

'I can't wait another thirty *years!*' I bellowed. My voice echoed around the cave, until Grandfather and both of my aunts were calling their own sleepy protests down the long tunnels of our home, but I ignored them. 'I can't live cooped up in this mountain forever, going nowhere, doing nothing –'

'*Jasper* is using his quiet years to teach himself philosophy.' Mother's voice no longer sounded weary; it grew cold and hard, like a diamond, as her neck stretched higher and higher above me, her giant golden eyes narrowing into dangerous slits focused solely on me, her disobedient daughter. 'Other dragons have found their own passions in literature, history or mathematics. Tell me, Aventurine: have you managed to find *your* passion yet?'

I ground my teeth together and scratched my front right claws through the piled gold beneath my feet. 'Lessons are boring. I want to explore and –'

'And how, exactly, do you plan to communicate with the creatures you meet on your explorations?' Mother asked sweetly. 'Or have you been progressing further with your language studies than I had imagined?'

Jasper let out a muffled snicker behind me. I swung around and shot a ball of smoke at him. He let it explode harmlessly in his face, his eyes gleaming with amusement.

'I can speak six languages already,' I muttered as I turned back to Mother.

Still, I couldn't quite lift my head to meet her gaze.

'By the time she was your age,' Mother said, 'your sister could speak and write twenty.'

'Hmmph.'

I didn't dare snort smoke at Mother. But I would have snorted it at Citrine if she had been stuck here with us, instead of living far away in her perfectly extraordinary, one-of-a-kind, dragon-sized palace. Citrine wrote epic poetry that filled other dragons with awe and was worshipped like a queen by every creature who came near her.

No one could measure up to my older sister. There was no point even trying.

I could feel Mother's gaze on me grow even sharper, as if she'd read my thoughts. 'Language,' she said, quoting one of Jasper's favourite philosophers, 'is a dragon's greatest power, reaching far beyond the realm of tooth and claw.'

'I know,' I muttered.

'Do you really, Aventurine?' Her long neck curved as her massive head swung down to look me in the eyes. 'Because courage is one thing, but recklessness is quite another. You may think yourself a ferocious beast, but outside this mountain you wouldn't survive a day. So you had better start being grateful that you have older and wiser relatives to look after you.'

Mother was sleeping deeply only two minutes later, her heavy breaths *whoosh*ing as calmly and evenly through the cavern as if we'd never even had an argument.

'Not a day?' Jasper whispered, once she was safely asleep. He shook off the last of the gemstones clinging to his back, and grinned at me, showing all of his teeth. 'Not an hour, more likely. Not even half an hour, knowing you.'

I glared at him, mantling my wings. 'I could look after myself perfectly well. I'm bigger and fiercer than anything else in these mountains.'

'But are you smarter?' He snorted. 'I'd wager all the gold in this cavern that even wolves are better at philosophical debates than you. And they probably don't set things on fire every time they lose!'

'Ohhh!' I whirled around, lashing my tail. But there was no escape. The cavern walls were too close, and feeling closer with every second. They were pushing in around me until I could barely breathe.

And I was supposed to spend another thirty years trapped inside this mountain, listening to my relatives tell me off for the fact that it was boring?

Never.

That was when I realised exactly what I had to do.

But I wasn't stupid, no matter what anyone thought. So I waited until Jasper finally gave up teasing me and curled up with one of his new human books – one that I hadn't burned. It was a philosophical tract, so I knew I would be safe.

'I'm going on a walk through the tunnels,' I told him, when he had flicked the pages five times with his claw.

'Mm-hmm,' Jasper murmured, without looking up. 'Aventurine, listen to this: this fellow thinks it's morally wrong to eat meat. And fish, too! He won't hurt any breathing creatures, so he only eats plants. Isn't that fascinating?'

'*Fascinating*? He's going to starve!' I flicked my ears in horror. 'I told you humans had pebbles for brains!'

But my brother didn't even hear me. Smoke trickled in a long, happy stream through his nostrils as he held the tiny book close to his eyes, rumbling with satisfaction.

I stepped right over his tail, one foot after another, on my way to freedom.

Rattling snores echoed down the long tunnels from the caverns where Grandfather Grenat, Aunt Tourmaline and Aunt Émeraude slept. Luckily, at this time of day, when the sun was at its highest, no one was likely to wake at a few scrabbling sounds from the corners of the mountain. Dropping to my belly, I wriggled my way up the side tunnel I'd discovered two years earlier, the one that was too small for any of the grown-ups to use. At the very top, filled and hidden by a boulder the size of my head, was a secret entrance to the mountain. It was my favourite spot in the world.

I'd shown Jasper of course, ages ago, but he almost never visited it – only when I dragged him there. He was always happiest curled up in our cavern with a book, or scratching out long, wordy treatises with one foreclaw dipped in ink.

I was the one who loved pushing the boulder free and poking the tip of my snout out of the hole, to take deep, tingling breaths of the fresh, outside air and watch the clouds float through the sky overhead. I'd never dared to go any further, but I lay there for hours sometimes, just dreaming of the day when I would finally be allowed to stretch my wings and fly across the endless sky.

Today, for the first time ever, I wasn't going to stop at dreaming.

I was going to show Jasper – *and* Mother – just how capable I was of taking care of myself. Then the grown-ups would have no excuse to keep me hidden away any longer.

With exhilaration flooding through me, I folded my wings tightly against my sides and lunged for the outside world and freedom.

It was harder than I'd expected to squeeze out of the hole. My shoulders stuck in the opening until I nearly roared with effort. I had to bite my mouth shut and swallow down choking smoke to keep myself silent. Finally, *finally*, I forced myself free with an explosive *pop!* It sent me tumbling on to the ground outside ... and whimpering with pain. My folded wings had scraped so hard against the rough, craggy edges of the rocks that there were ragged tears, now, in my silver and crimson scales.

What had Mother said? *'Your scales haven't hardened enough to withstand even a wolf's bite ...'*

I gnashed my teeth and pushed myself up on to all four feet, babying my wings by holding them half-folded at my side. Every breeze that blew across them made me wince, but I growled away the pain.

So, I wouldn't be making my first attempt at flight today. Never mind. I didn't need to fly to catch my prey.

For the first time in my life, the sky arched blue and free all around me, and I was free, too. The jagged peak of the mountain rose behind me. Below me lay a forested valley. And in between, buried somewhere in the rumpled foothills and narrow, rocky paths where animals and humans made their tiny ways ...

I set off down the mountainside, following the scent of food.

CHAPTER 2

Hunting wasn't nearly as easy as I'd expected.

The paths down the mountainside were made of scrabbly, rough earth that sent pebbles and balls of dirt skittering before me with every step. No matter how slowly and carefully I placed my feet, I couldn't stop those vicious little stones from flying ahead like spies racing to warn everyone that I was coming. By the time I'd been out for two full hours, I was ready to set the whole mountainside on fire ... and my stomach was growling louder than I was.

Again and again I heard birds calling, just begging to be eaten. Once I even smelt delicious warm-blooded animals slinking down the path barely fifty feet away. *So close!* But when I broke into a run to try to catch them off guard, the stream of pebbles turned into a flood beneath my feet, sending me slipping and sliding out of control into a cluster of scratchy pine trees ... and by the time I finally reached the spot where my prey had been gathering, they were long gone.

It was so unfair I couldn't bear it. I threw back my neck and shook with frustration. But I couldn't even let out a roar, in case my family heard me.

They would all be awake by now, inside the mountain. Of course they wouldn't think to look for me straight away. I'd often gone exploring in the tunnels before. But if I didn't come back soon, they'd start to wonder ... and if they found me before I'd managed to catch a single piece of food, I'd never be allowed out of our cavern again.

I couldn't go back empty-clawed, no matter what it took!

And that was when I heard a small male voice singing below me.

It had to be a human.

My nostrils flared. All my senses flamed into life as I picked out the scent of a warm, delicious mammal. Better yet, it was mixed with the smell of burning pine.

He'd lit a fire. He was sitting in one place.

And he was singing.

He would never hear me coming!

My muscles tensed in readiness, my haunches lowering into a preparatory crouch. But I didn't leap forward. Even I wasn't that reckless.

I might not love human books like Jasper did, but I'd still heard every one of Grandfather's stories.

What if this human had a musket? Or a sword?

Humans were a dragon's most dangerous prey. Even Mother didn't often hunt them by herself. Grandfather had taught us all to stay away from them whenever we were alone, to choose the safer, smarter meals ... and Grandfather had scales so strong they could deflect any blade or bullet.

I looked down at the tears in my aching wings and let out a low, unhappy rumble. Common sense felt like a boulder in my belly.

But then ...

Oh. My scales tingled as I suddenly imagined it: the look in Jasper's eyes as I carried a human into our cavern. Me. Myself. *On my own!*

Even Mother would have to admit I was ready to take care of myself in the outside world. There wasn't any better way to prove myself. I had to do it!

I sucked in a deep breath and lowered myself to the ground. Dirt and rocks rubbed against my belly as I crept forward. The human's voice never halted in his song, and as I grew closer and closer I started to make out the words, in a language that I recognised.

'... *And the winding road, oh the winding road, it never, ever stops ...*'

Ha! There were no roads in the world that didn't stop *somewhere.*

I'd *told* Jasper humans had pebbles for brains!

11

Finally, my prey came into sight. He'd found a sheltered hollow in the mountainside, surrounded on three sides by boulders and scrubby pine trees. In the centre he'd built a fire, and he was crouched over it now, with his back to me. As I peered through the trees I held my breath, clamping my mouth shut so that the hot smoke of my excitement couldn't escape and warn him.

He wasn't holding a sword or a musket. *Thank goodness.* And he wasn't one of those rare, dangerous humans who wielded magic – the worst kind of human trickery – because those ones wore fancy black coverings that made them look as if they had no legs. Grandfather had drawn a picture of one of them for me and Jasper, and he'd made us promise never to go anywhere near them until our protective scales were at least a hundred years hardened. This human, though, was dressed in perfectly safe layers of ragged purple and pink cloth that showed his skinny limbs quite clearly.

Still, if this was going to work, I had to be *fast.* Too fast for him to yank out a sword or a bow and arrow from that big bag that sat beside him … or an axe, or …

I'm bigger than him and fiercer than him, I told myself sternly. *I'm the scariest creature on this mountain.*

Then he started to turn in my direction.

Now! I opened my mouth in a silent roar and *leaped.*

'Aaargh!' The human screamed and dropped whatever he'd been holding into the pot. He lurched backwards, tripped on a rock and fell on to his backside as I bounded triumphantly towards him.

Then I screamed, too, as my injured wings scraped against the half circle of pine trees on the way. 'Aaargh!'

I fell short, lunging away from the pain, and landed hard just next to the fire, clutching my wings to my side. '*Ow, ow, ow!*'

Oops. As the human's eyes widened, I realised I'd said that out loud.

'Raaar!' I drew myself up and bared all fifty teeth. *That's better.* The human blinked hard, sweat popping up across his face. He opened his mouth, but no sound came out.

Towering over him, I prepared to lunge.

And that was when I smelt it.

Luscious, sweet, exotic flavour. Rich and blooming and steaming *just beneath my nose.*

I snaked my long neck towards the fire with lethal speed. 'What is *that*?'

'Wh-wh-what?' The human pushed himself another foot backwards, staring at me.

I ignored his retreat. Time enough to catch him later. All I cared about right now was the pot he had set over the fire, the pot whose steam was reaching out and tickling my senses with something so amazing my mouth was already watering. I *had to have it!*

The pot was full of boring boiling water, but it swirled with brown tendrils as more and more of something dark and chunky dissolved into it.

'What did you put in this pot?' I demanded.

'That?' He stopped moving. 'That's chocolate.'

'*Chocolate?*' I'd never heard of chocolate before. Jasper

had never mentioned it, and he'd read every work of human philosophy that he could get his claws on. How could his philosophers get so excited about eating *plants* when something this delicious was available?

I lowered my snout as close to the pot as I dared without knocking it over. Then I took a long, deep breath through my nose.

Oh, heaven.

A low growl of yearning rumbled through me, filling the clearing. 'This is *chocolate*?'

Until now all I'd ever wanted was meat, whether it was scorched or raw or lightly toasted. I'd assumed that there couldn't be anything better. But now ...

Was this how Jasper felt about his philosophy?

I had to know how chocolate tasted. I couldn't go another moment without that knowledge! I angled my neck just right, leaned forward, and ...

'Wait!' The human jumped up.

I reared back in disbelief. 'Did you just say *wait* to me?' Outrage sent my injured wings flaring as I stared down at him. He was puny and insignificant, and he was trying to *keep me from my chocolate*?

'I'm going to have to eat you first after all,' I said sadly.

'No!' He darted in front of me, his hands held high. 'I just meant the chocolate isn't ready yet. It's supposed to be *hot* chocolate. I haven't finished mixing it all together. I haven't even added any spices!'

I narrowed my eyes at him. 'You mean it gets even better than this?'

'You've never had hot chocolate before, have you?' he said.

'Well ...' I thought back to Grandfather's warnings about tricksy humans. 'I might have,' I said slyly. 'You never know.'

He hesitated a moment. Then he leaned down and scooped up a wooden spoon from the ground, his hand trembling. 'Trust me,' he said. 'You should have the full experience.'

Before I could answer, he turned away from me and began to stir.

Watching him carefully, I settled on my haunches to wait.

As his face squeezed tight with concentration, he began to whisper to himself, almost chanting the words. Was he singing that stupid song again? The rhythms didn't sound quite the same, but who needed to hear more human nonsense? Not me. I didn't even try to make it out.

The moment he reached into his pocket, though, I grabbed his shoulder with one claw. 'No swords!'

'I – I ...' He stuttered to a halt. 'It's not a sword,' he finally managed. 'Look.' He pulled out a bag from his pocket. 'It's just cinnamon.'

Cinnamon? I leaned down towards the bag suspiciously. If he was trying to poison me ...

'I'll eat some myself,' he said. 'Look.' He reached one shaking finger into the bag and scooped out a few orangey-brown specks. Then he swallowed them. 'See?'

I *smelt*, which was even better. The open bag smelt amazing.

'Put it in,' I ordered. I wanted to smell that combination. I could already tell that the mixture of cinnamon and chocolate would be *wonderful*.

He shook in a few pinches, breathing hard.

Ohhhh, I had been right. These new smells were *even better*.

I was almost starting to wish that I didn't have to take him home afterwards for my family to eat. It would be much more satisfying to keep this human as a pet, to make hot chocolate for me any time I wanted.

He would be a hard-working pet, too, I could tell. As he stirred the hot chocolate, he kept on whispering to himself the whole time in that funny rhythmic chant, his whole body taut with concentration. I suppose I could have listened harder, to try to pick out his words, but really, when had I ever cared about anything that humans said? Besides, I was far too busy enjoying the smells from his pot. If I could have, I would have wrapped myself up in those steamy tendrils of scent and rolled around in them for hours. *Hot chocolate*. Talk about a treasure fit for a dragon!

I'd have to look for more chocolate in his luggage when I finished here. I already knew I would have to have hot chocolate again. *Lots* of it.

Finally, he looked up and gave me a nervous, wavering smile. 'It's ready,' he said. 'Shall I pour it into a cup, or ...'

I snorted, sending a ball of smoke flying past his face. 'Do you really think I could drink from one of your tiny human cups?'

'I suppose not,' he said. 'You'd better drink it from the pot then.' He wrapped one soft, human hand in his outer covering for protection, and then lifted the pot by its long handle. 'Look out, it's hot.'

I gave him a contemptuous look as I reached out with one forefoot. 'I'm a *dragon*.'

My claws curved around the little pot, cradling it like the most precious of gems. Carefully, I lifted it to my mouth. Closing my eyes, I tipped the luxuriant, hot liquid into my mouth.

Ohhhhh!

Bliss exploded through my senses. I reeled with pleasure.

Chocolate chocolate chocolate –

'Ahhhh!'

And then everything exploded inside me, and the world went black.

CHAPTER 3

The first thing I realised when my eyes opened was that I was in the wrong place. Just a moment ago I'd been sitting on my haunches, looking down at that colourfully dressed human with the astonishing cooking skills. Now all I could see was blue sky.

Oh. I must be lying on my back.

Well, that was strange. I'd never lain on my back before. It would have crushed my wings.

My wings! Where were my wings? I couldn't feel them underneath me. I scrambled to get back on all four legs – and promptly fell on to my front.

What was wrong with my legs?

I opened my mouth to let the smoke free from my throat. Then I realised: there wasn't any. Why wasn't there any smoke building up in my throat? I always coughed up smoke when I panicked. And I was definitely panicking now!

'Careful,' said a voice nearby. It sounded familiar, but not quite right. The last time I'd heard that voice, it had sounded so much smaller.

I twisted my neck around. It was surprisingly hard to do. But I didn't have time to worry about that.

The creature standing before me was human. It was *my* human. But how had he got so big? A minute ago he'd been tiny. Now he towered over me.

'You should move slowly,' he told me. 'It'll take you a while to adjust, I expect.'

'Adjust to *what*?' I shrieked.

Then I froze, my throat closing up in protest. That hadn't been my voice. *My* voice was supposed to thunder through the clearing. *This* voice sounded tiny and creaky. It sounded ... it sounded almost like ...

Shivers seized my body and shook it against the ground.

'Here.' The human sighed and pulled the outer layer of cloth off his arms and back. 'You look cold. It's probably from shock.' He dropped the long purple thing over my back, and it flooded across me, falling to the ground on both sides.

How could it be so big on me? Unless ...

'I can't be,' I whispered, in that terrible, small, wrong voice. 'No!'

'Oh yes,' he said. 'I am sorry, you know, but it couldn't be helped. You were going to eat me, after all ... and when you were that size, I had no hope of stopping you.' He moved his shoulders up and down. 'What else could I do but fix that?'

The world spun around me. I couldn't breathe. I tried to dig my claws into the dirt to steady myself. They pushed uselessly against it and refused to sink in.

I would not look down to see the reason why. I kept my gaze on the lying, deceiving human in front of me.

'You're not a magic person!' I said. 'You can't fool me. You're not wearing black coverings!'

'Black – ? Ohhh, I know what you mean. You're thinking of the king's battle mages in their robes.' He snorted. 'No, I'm not one of *them*. They do all the big, flashy magic on the battlefields, so they get all the gold and glory, and the uniform, too. But as for me ...'

His lips stretched into a smug smile. 'I'm something far more interesting: a food mage. There aren't many of us, but trust me, we're not lacking in power. And you liked the hot chocolate that I enchanted, didn't you? So that's something.'

Something? That hot chocolate had been the best thing I had ever tasted. Just the memory of it made my stomach hurt with longing.

After all of Mother's worries, I had finally found my passion ... but at the worst possible moment.

And what exactly did he mean by *enchanted*?

The food mage leaned down and scooped out something round from his bag. It glinted in the sunlight. Dread filled my stomach. I knew what that was. Grandfather had brought one home for us once, along with a whole batch of other human contraptions like kettles and pots for us to study. Citrine had identified it immediately.

A *mirror*.

'Do you want to see yourself?' he asked with a strange gentleness.

No, I thought. But I wouldn't let myself say it out loud. I was a dragon. I would not act afraid of anything, especially not in front of someone who should have been my prey.

The mirror came closer and closer as I lay, frozen, waiting for it.

I would not run. I would not disgrace myself. I ...

He lowered the mirror directly in front of my face.

A very young human female looked back at me with wide, horrified, golden eyes.

The food mage didn't stay long after that. Whistling, he gathered together all his things, taking the time to wipe down his cooking pot. My mouth watered at the smell, but I clamped my small, blunt teeth together and forced myself not to ask for any more of his chocolate.

He didn't deserve that satisfaction.

'Change. Me. Back!' I ordered him. '*Or else!*'

Fifteen minutes earlier he would have trembled at the growl that rumbled through my voice. Now he only gave me a twisted smile as he slung his bag over his shoulder. 'Good luck, little dragon.'

He'd taken back his outer covering by then, leaving me wearing only what the transformation had left me, a silver-and-crimson fabric in the pattern of my scales. It covered my raw, unscaled body like a second skin, but it left my soft feet completely unprotected. No matter how hard I tried, I couldn't force myself to look closely at those poor, bare little things, or at the silver-and-crimson imitations of my scales. Whenever I tried, my pathetic teeth chattered against each other uncontrollably, and I had to wrap my weak upper limbs around my chest to keep the rest of me still.

Grandfather will know what to do. I just had to keep repeating that to myself every time I started to forget that dragons never, ever got scared.

'You might come to like being human, you know,' said the food mage. 'Once you get over the surprise of it all, you should travel down the mountain. The closest city is Drachenburg, the capital. That's probably the best place to find a livelihood and a place to stay.'

'A *livelihood*?' I repeated, and stared at him. 'What's that?'

Sighing, he shook his head. 'You have a lot to learn. Just remember: go that way.' He pointed down the mountainside. 'I'd look for a position as an apprentice, if I were you. I don't know how old you were as a dragon, but you don't look more than twelve now, so you're about the right age. You'd better start walking soon, though. You don't want to be stuck up here in the dark when the wild animals come out.'

'I'm the fiercest thing in these mountains!' I snarled.

He made a funny little noise in the back of his throat.

Then the furry lines over his eyes lowered. His mouth twisted. There was something about his face ... oh, stones and bones. Was that *pity* I saw?

How I wished that I still had the power to breathe flames! I would have set him alight, chocolate and all, just to wipe that expression out of existence.

'Good luck,' he repeated, and turned away.

A minute later, even the sound of his whistling had faded. I was alone in the clearing, on a mountain that suddenly felt enormous.

Right. Fury gave me power. Gritting my teeth together, I rolled over and pushed my back feet into the ground.

I can do this.

I hadn't dared try to stand up in front of the food mage. I couldn't bear for anyone – especially *him* – to witness me wobbling around like a fool. Now that he was gone, though, I wasn't going to stay here a moment longer. I had a mountain to climb and – I groaned at the thought of it, sagging back down on to all fours – I had a horrible surprise for my family.

Oh, how my mother and my grandfather and both of my aunts were going to shake their heads over me when they saw what had happened! My puny teeth clenched at the thought of what they would say. And the way Jasper would tease me afterwards ...

Never mind. I just had to get it over with as quickly as possible, and then – once all the thundering and wing-flaring was past – they'd settle down and sort me back into my proper form.

Somehow.

But dragons can't do magic, whispered a tiny, high-pitched voice in the back of my mind.

I silenced it immediately, growling low in my short, narrow throat. I wasn't about to lower my neck in submission and give up. I was a dragon, not a worm, and it was time to return to my cave. For once I would happily sit back and let my family take care of everything until this ludicrous little problem was fixed.

And then I would find more chocolate! All I had to do, first, was learn to walk.

If humans could do it, how hard could it be? I shoved myself upright with a grunt of effort.

Five minutes later, I was panting and lying on the ground again, where I'd fallen hard ... *again*. Human bodies were ridiculous!

Snarling, I slammed my forefeet – *hands* – on to the ground.

I couldn't walk on two legs? Fine! I'd just walk on all fours then. It made far more sense anyway. Humans would do it themselves if they were more practical creatures. All it took was a little cleverness, angling my over-long back legs in just the right way, and then ...

O*www!* Whimpering, I dropped back down to the ground after only three steps and sucked my hurting right hand in my mouth for comfort. A drop of blood leaked on to my tongue.

Ick! I spat it out in horror. How could *blood* not taste good?

24

This spell really had gone right through me. If I didn't get it fixed soon, I'd end up craving vegetables!

That was more than enough to make me try again.

This time I wriggled around until I found a fallen branch lying not too far away. *There!* I'd heard of dragons who managed with only three feet. If they could do it, so could I.

Gritting my teeth, I started to limp-walk up the mountainside.

After twenty minutes I managed to toss the stick aside and walk – not easily, but capably – on two sore and aching feet.

After thirty minutes a massive shadow passed overhead. I jerked my head back so fast that my neck *poinged* in protest.

Aha!

Up above me, where there should have been nothing but blue sky gradually fading into darkness, I saw a massive expanse of red and gold, flying low and close, barely higher than the treeline.

I would have recognised that scale pattern anywhere.

'Grandfather!' I yelled. I started jumping up and down, finding new muscles in my human legs that I hadn't even felt before. I waved my arms wildly, giddy with relief. 'Grandfather, it's me!'

His head – so much huger from this position! – tilted. One great golden eye focused on my jumping figure.

'Grandfather!' I yelled again.

He gathered his wings and circled around to fly ... in the opposite direction.

My mouth dropped open. I stared up at him in disbelief.

'Hey!' I yelled. I reached down and grabbed a rock the size of my hand. 'Come back here!'

I threw the rock as hard as I could.

It didn't hit him, of course. It fell far short. But it caught his attention, just as I'd hoped it would.

His neck snaked around in a whirl of colour. His enormous mouth opened wide.

I put both hands to my tiny human mouth. 'Grandfa–!'

Flame billowed out of his mouth in a massive fireball aimed straight at me.

My new body took over before my mind could catch up with it. I fell to the ground and tumbled hard, tucking my head into my chest and wrapping myself into a ball.

Heat scorched my back, then disappeared. I lay frozen, waiting for the next fireball to arrive.

Without my scales I would burn to ashes in seconds.

Any moment now …

Wait. How long had it been?

Warily, I opened my eyes.

Slowly, I untucked my head.

Far away, in the sky above, I saw the distant figure of my grandfather flapping away from me. He didn't even bother to look back.

I stared after him.

He'd tried to flame me.

And then he'd left me here!

Family never left each other. Dragons protected their

hoards and their hatchlings with their lives! It didn't matter how much I complained about all the bossy adults in my mountain, I knew with every fibre of my being that they'd do anything – anything! – to keep me safe.

But then ... My human throat swallowed convulsively again and again, as if something horrible was caught inside ... like the truth.

... I wasn't their hatchling any more, was I?

My gaze clung to my grandfather's figure as he grew smaller and smaller in the distance. Bruises and scratches covered my soft, weak limbs, making every inch of my skin ache.

I knew exactly what my grandfather had seen when he'd looked down at me.

That fireball had only been a warning. He wouldn't bother to actually kill a pesky little human unless she did something really provocative and threatening, something like ... oh, say, *trying to make my way into the family cavern.*

Taking a deep breath, I pushed myself up until I was sitting on my padded backside on the hard ground, my arms wrapped defensively around my legs. The air was cooling as the sky darkened. A strong breeze blew across the mountain, fluttering my long, black head-fur around my face and sending chills rippling through my vulnerable, unscaled skin.

The mountainside spread out below me, just as it had four hours earlier when I'd first set out on my grand adventure.

But this time I finally understood that I couldn't go home again.

CHAPTER 4

Without my flame, I couldn't even start a fire. All I had to keep me warm through that long night was the shelter of a rock and my own horrible thoughts ... oh, and my growling stomach, too.

Inside the mountain, Jasper and Mother, Grandfather and my aunts were all sleeping on cosy mounds of gold and jewels with trails of warm smoke ruffling out of their noses. Every time I pictured their comfortable sleep, I snarled ... but only because snarling was better than moaning.

I had never felt so small or so pathetic in my life.

But then, I'd never lost my family before.

By the time the sun finally began to rise, though, I was sick and tired of my misery. I'd thrown dozens of rocks the evening before, smashing them into the mountainside until my stringy human muscles had burned with effort. Then I'd felt strange wet drops stream out of my tiny human eyes for hours as I lay huddled on the cold ground, giving in to my weakness in the dark, where no one could witness the humiliation.

Now I was finished. *No more!* I blinked out the last of the irritating wetness from my aching eyes and pushed myself up from the ground with a growl of fury. What kind of dragon would curl up and surrender just because she'd had a bit of bad luck? My family might not think I could survive on my own, but I would show them. I would show everyone, including that lying, cheating food mage, exactly how strong I really was. I would walk my way down this mountain, I would find myself a *livelihood*, whatever that might mean ... and I would eat as much chocolate as I wanted, *forever*!

I'd made it all the way off the mountain and on to the wide dirt track that cut through the green, wooded lower foothills before I heard hoof-beats coming up behind me. My soft, unprotected feet hurt so badly by then that pain thudded through me with each new step and I had to clench every muscle to force myself through it. I hardly even noticed the steady clopping sounds growing closer.

But when I heard the sound of two voices raised enthusiastically in song, my shoulders hunched in agonised protest.

Not that winding-road song again! Nothing good ever happened when I heard that song!

Worse yet, now that I could make out more of the words, they made even less sense than the verse that the food mage had sung.

'*For true friends can never, ever be parted, and true love can never be stopped when it's started ...*'

Oh no? I growled low in my human throat. *Try getting transformed into the wrong species and see how fast you get parted from your friends, humans!*

As the hoof-beats and the caterwauling drew closer, I braced myself and turned to see exactly what was coming towards me.

Oooh! As I sucked in a breath of longing, my stomach growled louder than ever. The hoof-beats belonged to a big white horse who made my mouth water at the sight of him. What a fine meal he would have made for a dragon!

The humans behind him were well padded, too, and wrapped in loose, dark green outer coverings, with more saggy green fabric plopped on top of their heads. I'd never seen a dragon with only one colour in their scales, but maybe these humans were hoping to be mistaken for trees. If so, they were much too noisy for the trick to work. They rode high in a jangly cart, but even the rattling of its wheels and the horse's hoof-beats couldn't drown out their non-sensical song.

Then they saw me.

'Oh, oh, oh!' The female grabbed the male's arm. 'Friedrich, look, it's a girl! Oh, stop now, stop!'

Oh yes, I agreed silently. *Please let the singing stop!*

But the humans didn't just stop singing. The male

tugged on the straps that he held in his hands, and the horse drew to a stop only two feet away from me, whiffling suspiciously.

Ah, the frustration of having tiny, blunt human teeth! But I was still a dragon inside, where it mattered. I tipped my head back to meet the horse's gaze and let him see it: yes, he was right to be suspicious. I was a predator. If I'd had my claws and fire right now, he'd be the best breakfast I'd ever had.

'Oh, you poor child!'

Ack! I should have been paying more attention to the animals behind the horse.

I staggered back in horror, but it was too late. The female human had already jumped down from the cart and thrown her arms around me. She pressed my face into her soft chest until I could barely breathe.

'Just look at you! Wandering in this terrible wilderness all alone. I can scarcely believe it! Oh, Friedrich, look, she doesn't even have any shoes! And she can't be more than twelve, can she? Oh, she is just exactly what we've been looking for!'

Shoes? What were shoes? And how could they possibly have known to look for me? Even I hadn't known I would be here.

But I couldn't have asked her any questions if I had wanted to. My mouth was smushed against her fuzzy green covering, and my arms were pinned to my sides.

'Mmmmph!' I managed, through closed lips. 'Mmph!'

'Oh, you're *cold*,' the female said. 'Look, Friedrich, she's cold, and she doesn't have anyone to look after her, so really we'd be doing her a favour, now, wouldn't we? We couldn't possibly leave her here like this, could we? Oh no, no, you're quite right. It's really for the best for all of us.'

Had Friedrich said anything? All I'd heard from him so far was a muffled sigh as he sat on the high seat of the cart, keeping his gaze steadily fixed away from us. But my captor started forward as if he'd agreed with her, tugging me towards the cart, pulling off her green covering and wrapping it around my shoulders. It trailed to the ground and pooled around me, so warm that I couldn't bring myself to push it off again.

Still, I dug in my bleeding feet and slapped my hands against the cart before she could actually pick me up and put me into it. 'Wait!'

'Wait?' The female blinked rapidly at me, her mouth making an O. 'Oh, Friedrich, she's upset. Why is she so upset? Do you think she's frightened? Or –'

Friedrich still didn't turn to look at us, but his face scrunched up underneath his bushy grey face-fur as if he was in pain. 'Now, Greta –'

But I didn't need anyone to speak for me. 'I am *not* frightened of anything or anybody!' I drew myself up to my full height and glared up at the human who'd trapped me. 'Where exactly do you think you're taking me? I don't even know if you're going in the right direction!'

'The right *what*?' she said. 'You're on your own in the middle of the *mountains*! How could anything be the wrong direction from here?'

But for the first time Friedrich turned around. ''S a fair question, Greta.' He nodded down at me from his seat on the cart. 'Where are you headed, young lady?'

I tilted my chin up proudly. 'I'm going to a big city,' I said, 'to find a livelihood.'

'You want to work?' Greta said. 'Oh, isn't that wonderful? You see, we have the perfect position for you already.' She beamed. 'If you could believe it, we've just lost our last maid. That girl was so unreasonable and greedy – *such* a city girl! She was always demanding to be paid for every little thing she did, always whining about wanting days off ... Oh, she broke my heart with her ingratitude, she really did. Didn't she, Friedrich?'

Friedrich's eyes rolled around so wildly I took a step back. Was this a human warning signal? Was he about to attack?

Greta didn't seem to have noticed, but then, she was looking at me, not at him. 'Now here you are, like a miracle, to take her place,' she said happily. 'It was obviously meant to be! We'll take you into our home just as if you were our own daughter, and you can cook and clean and do all the little things we need, and of course you won't need any payment at all, will you, because you would have starved if we'd left you here, so really –'

'No cleaning,' I said firmly. Friedrich's eyes had stopped rolling, but I kept a wary piece of my attention on him as I spoke, just in case. 'And I won't be a maid, whatever that is. I'm going to be an *apprentice*, and I need to find chocolate.'

'Chocolate?' Greta stepped back, blinking rapidly. 'You?'

Friedrich's big shoulders rose and fell under his green covering. 'Plenty of chocolate houses in Drachenburg nowadays,' he said. 'It's the new fashion, isn't it? King's fancy.'

'Hmmph,' said Greta. 'As if you'd ever stepped into a chocolate house in your life, Friedrich. Honestly, the things you say! If you didn't have me to look after you ...'

But I had already made up my mind. 'Perfect,' I said.

A house made of chocolate? What could be better? I couldn't wait to move into one now that I was human!

Then I frowned, remembering danger. 'There aren't any food mages in those chocolate houses, are there?'

Greta stared at me with enormous greyish-green eyes. Then she burst into laughter. 'You really are an ignorant little creature, aren't you?' Smiling, she stepped back up to me and rubbed the top of my head, mussing up all my head-fur and making my teeth clench. 'Why, I've never heard of a real food mage in my life! Honestly, I think they're just a myth, like music mages. Magic doesn't happen around respectable folk, you know!'

Phew. I jerked away before she could rub my head again, but I was too relieved to snarl.

The next time I ate chocolate, it was definitely going to be non-magical! I'd had quite enough unexpected transformations for a lifetime.

'What about other kinds of mages?' I asked. 'Are there many of those in Drachenburg?' If I could intimidate one into helping me ...

Friedrich shrugged, adjusting the horse's long leather straps in his hands. 'There's always the king's battle mages,' he said. '*They're* real enough, aren't they? There are probably around a dozen of those, gathered up from all across the kingdom and all living together near the palace, so I've heard. Ready to be sent out to fight enemies and dragons and suchlike on the king's command. Like in the storybooks, you know. Excitement.' He slid a glance at Greta, who was looking at him with narrowed eyes, and added hastily, 'Not that I would want it for myself, of course.'

'Hmmph.' I scowled.

I had a strong suspicion that any mages who specialised in fighting dragons would be completely unreasonable about turning me back *into* one, no matter how fair and just that would be. Besides, there was no point in being transformed back into my proper shape only to be immediately captured by a bunch of dragon-hating battle mages.

'All right,' I said, and turned in the direction that the horse was facing. *Towards chocolate.* 'I'll go to Drachenburg then.'

'With us!' said Greta, clapping her hands. 'That's where we live!'

'Well ...' Frowning, I started to back away. I didn't like the determined look in her eyes. 'I'm not sure ...'

'There's no point arguing with her,' Friedrich told me, and shifted over on the bench of the cart. 'Might as well get in now, save us all the bother.'

'And isn't it lucky for you that we were here to help?' Greta wrapped her arm around my shoulder, halting me in my retreat. 'We would never ordinarily be out in the wilds, you know, but we were just visiting my sister and her husband on their farm.'

Gently, she began to tug, pulling me slowly back towards the cart as her words streamed brightly over my head. 'If you can believe it, those two are both so provincial they have no idea how much everything really costs in Drachenburg. They're *such* nitwits when it comes to money! So we always pick up plenty of cheap fresh food from them and then sell it for a wonderful profit back in Drachenburg. Really, it only serves them right for being so foolish, doesn't it?' She gave a little rippling laugh. 'Although we do keep some of it for ourselves, of course. You can never get *really* good milk or meat in the city, can you?'

My head was whirling from her stream of words, and I didn't even know what 'milk' was. But at the word 'meat', my stomach gave an almost dragonish roar.

'Just listen to you! You're starving!' Greta scooped me up with surprisingly strong arms, hefting me into the cart before I could protest. 'And just look at all that blood on your bare feet. Here ...' She climbed up after me, then leaned over the seat, digging into the bags and baskets and boxes that were all stacked precariously in the back of the cart, as Friedrich clicked his tongue and the horse started forward. 'I don't have any shoes in here, but at least I can give you some food for the journey.'

'Meat?' I said hopefully. I craned my short neck, trying to see into the basket she was digging through.

'*Meat?*' She let out a burble of laughter. 'Lord, child, we can't stop and build a fire to cook meat now! We're still in sight of the mountains, aren't we? Don't you know how dangerous it is out here? We like to roll through just as quickly as we can, don't we, Friedrich?'

'But I don't need my meat cooked,' I said. 'Really!'

'Oh, you silly thing, I can see how hungry you are, but don't worry. You don't need to resort to that. Just look what I found.' Greta popped back up with a beaming smile that showed all of her teeth, while she kept her hands hidden under her green covering. 'Ta-da!' She pulled out one hand. 'A bottle of milk, fresh from my sister's best cow! And –' she pulled out her other hand – 'goat's cheese!'

I stared at them in horror.

The milk was white. Bone-white. So was the cheese. If they were meat, they would have been rancid.

'Are you sure they're safe?' I asked.

'What a question!' Shaking her head, Greta unscrewed the lid from the bottle. 'You think I'm going to let you starve before we even get you to the city? Especially when you're going to be such a good, grateful child from now on and do every little thing we ask of you?'

'What?' I said. 'I'm not –'

'Here you go!' She pushed the open bottle into my face until I had no choice but to drink or let it pour down my chin.

I drank. And then I kept on drinking, because she didn't let up the pressure. I didn't finally manage to push it away until I'd had two long gulps. *Phew*. Before I could recover, I found a slab of clammy white cheese in my hand.

'Eat up!' Greta said brightly, and pushed it towards my mouth. 'You'll need your strength soon enough!'

My stomach twisted at the sight, but I gave in.

Humans ate the strangest things. Luckily, my new human body apparently did, too. The cheese didn't hurt my throat or stomach at all. Neither did the milk. I wasn't even disgusted by the taste.

My grandfather would have been so ashamed of me.

But I was definitely drawing the line at vegetables.

Greta watched me with an almost draconic eye until I'd eaten every crumb of cheese and drunk the very last sip of milk. Then she gave a contented sigh. 'There. You'll be all right now, won't you? I'll wrap up your feet to keep you from bleeding on the cart, and then you'll be ready to set to work just as soon as we get home.'

I wiped off the last drops of milk from my chin and gave her a wary look. I'd always known humans had tiny brains, but this one seemed particularly forgetful.

'I'm going to work in a *chocolate house*,' I reminded her. 'I'm not going to be your maid – or anyone else's. Remember?'

'Oh, of course, of course,' she murmured. 'How could I forget? Now just sit back and let us take care of everything until we reach the city ... because, trust me, you'd never find it on your own.' She patted my shoulder. 'You're just lucky we came across you out here. Do you know –' her voice dropped as she leaned even closer to me, squeezing me tightly between her and Friedrich – 'my cousin Georg saw a dragon flying over these mountains once! They say there's a whole nest of those vicious creatures living around here.'

'Now, Greta ...' Friedrich sounded weary.

'I'm serious!' Greta said. 'Oh, no one likes to talk about them, but they do exist, you know. There's no point pretending otherwise. They may stay clear of the big cities and farms nowadays, but anyone who travels in these mountains is in danger. Why, I suffer from the terror of it every time we travel! Don't I, Friedrich?'

Friedrich only heaved a heavy sigh. But I thought I saw the horse's ears flick in irritation. I didn't blame him.

'I don't know why the king lets them stay here,' Greta said. 'I keep saying and saying, he ought to send out his battle mages to finish them all off for good! I know I'd sleep better at night. And there are a lot of important people in the city who agree with me!'

'Finish off *dragons*?' I couldn't stay quiet any longer. I jerked my head around to glare at her. 'Are you crazy?'

Her mouth fell open. 'Well, of all the rude things to say!'

I scowled. 'Those dragons would eat every one of the battle mages if they tried.'

'That's what I said,' Friedrich muttered. 'The king's a sensible man, Greta. He doesn't want to get near any dragons. No one does.'

Well, I did. I would have given anything to get back to my family, especially right at that moment.

But the cart carried me further and further away from our cavern with every *clip-clop* of the horse's big feet, as Friedrich and Greta argued over exactly how best to deal with dragons, whether it was poisoning or spell-casting, staying well out of their way (Friedrich's idea) or sending in the whole army to kill them (as if they could).

And then, unbelievably, things got even worse. Because when the arguing finally stopped, Greta decided it was time for another jolly round of travel songs.

It was going to be a very long journey.

CHAPTER 5

By the time we'd been travelling for over an hour, my head was nodding to one side and my backside was aching on the cart's wooden bench. Greta had finished wrapping up my injured feet in cloth and was busy rolling her eyes in despair over how ignorant I was about what she called 'clothing'.

If I'd still been in my proper form, I would have snorted out gallons of smoke at the very idea of caring about what humans chose to put on their little bodies. As it was, I was horribly certain that the information was going to actually matter to me soon. Unfortunately, after my sleepless night on the mountainside, I had to jerk myself upright again and again to stay awake for Greta's condescending lecture.

The sixth time that I shook myself awake, she heaved an exasperated sigh and tucked my head against her shoulder with a firm hand.

'There, there,' she murmured. 'You just let yourself sleep until we get there. It's better that way for all of us, isn't it?'

'Mmm,' I mumbled.

There was something niggling in the back of my mind, but I couldn't catch hold of it. Some kind of warning, if I could only remember ...

But it was too late. The moment my eyes closed, I was swept away in the darkness into dreams of gleaming gold and jewels. I was laughing as I chased after Jasper, spilling jingling treasure everywhere as I pounced on him ... I was tearing into fresh, delicious meat that my family had just brought back from their hunt ... I was listening to Grandfather laugh and laugh as Jasper and I –

'*Aventurine!*' It was Grandfather's warning, the one I'd heard so many times. How could I have forgotten it even for a moment? '*Never trust a human. They lie and cheat!*'

I jerked awake, my heart thudding against my chest. My breathing felt fast and tight, as if I'd been running for hours.

And I was surrounded by humans, *everywhere*.

Tall, rectangular buildings reached towards the sky to my right and to my left and marched on in rows and rows ahead of me, as far as my eyes could follow. Humans carrying baskets and bags bustled in crowds along the pavement on each side of the stony street and yammered noisily to each other in the horse-drawn carts that rattled past in a non-stop procession. I was so hemmed in I could hardly breathe.

How could all the humans stand it?

The hills that we'd been travelling through when I first fell asleep rose high in the distance now, beyond a tall stone tower with a massive clock face that overlooked the busy human city, ticking away all the hours that I'd lost. It couldn't have been later than nine in the morning when I'd first closed my eyes. Now it looked more like mid-afternoon.

And I didn't like the look of where those hours had carried me.

Our cart had rolled to a stop in front of a tall red-brick building, with scattered squares of clear glass dotted around its front and pots of pink flowers clustered before them. From the flowers to the sickly-sweet figurines set in front of the house's entryway, it looked exactly like the sort of place where Greta would live ... but I didn't spot a single piece of chocolate anywhere.

I didn't smell any chocolate either.

As my senses prickled with danger, I heard Greta whisper to Friedrich over my head, 'Now, *stop* being so stubborn and just carry her inside! I *know* what she said, but by the time she wakes up, it'll all be sorted, and –'

'I'm awake!' I snarled, and sat bolt upright. I would have spread out my wings and arched my neck if I could, to make myself as big and dangerous-looking as possible. Instead I narrowed my eyes into a glower as I looked from one of my treacherous companions to the other. 'This isn't a chocolate house, is it?'

Friedrich winced and slid off the seat of the cart, turning his gaze away as if he couldn't bear to watch. But Greta smiled and wrapped her fingers around my shoulder, squeezing so tightly that I couldn't escape.

As I looked into her eyes I realised something that I'd almost forgotten on our long journey: even without any claws or scales, humans had always been predators, too.

'Now, dear ...' Her fingers tightened even more, pinching into my skin, as she leaned towards me. 'I know you *think* you want to work in a chocolate house, but trust me, you wouldn't last a day in one of those fine places. Why, you didn't even know what shoes were until I told you! Really, no one but us would even want to hire you. And without us, you would have starved all alone in the wild!

'So now that we've brought you all the way here, and even shared our own food and drink out of the pure generosity of our hearts –' she nudged me gently towards where Friedrich stood on the other side of the cart, his face tilted away from us and his shoulders sagging – 'it's time for you to be a good, obedient girl and pay us back. You just hop down next to Friedrich and we'll all go inside where it's safe, through that door right there –' she pointed – 'and you won't ever have to worry about taking care of yourself again. Do you understand, dear?'

I looked into Greta's smiling face, as her hard fingers gripped my frail human shoulder through the thick green covering she'd lent me, and I smiled back at her.

It was a smile that showed all my teeth, and my family would have recognised it in an instant.

'I understand,' I said sweetly.

'Good girl.' Her fingers finally loosened ...

... And I leaped straight off the cart, leaving her dull green covering behind me.

I landed hard on the city street, a full foot away from where Friedrich waited. Sighing, he shifted towards me.

He was too late.

Tucking my head down, I spun around and ran as fast as my legs would take me, weaving past carts and horses and humans alike.

I'd left one safe, smothering cavern behind already.

I was never going to let myself be trapped again.

Muck and horse dung covered the round, bumpy stones of the city streets, forming a stinky, sticky mess and turning my cloth-covered feet gooey within seconds. Only twenty minutes after my great escape, I had to stop running so that I could scrape off my foot-coverings for the fifth time.

To keep my balance I hung on to a thick, cream-coloured artificial tree trunk that had been set into the pavement, with one of the humans' fancy glass lamps balanced at the top of it. It was a funny thing to put in the middle of a city, but it wasn't the strangest thing I saw as I looked around me.

Tall yellow-and-white buildings rose on both sides of the street, embellished like jewellery with fluttery, swirly ornamentation and dotted with rows and rows of thin glass rectangles. Crowds of humans flooded in and out of the open doorways, chatting and laughing and filling their arms with more and more bags and decorated boxes.

Greta's home had been halfway up a street of red-brick houses, with every door shut tight against the world. The scene around me now was so different that if I hadn't seen the same massive, forested green foothills rising in the distance, and the same giant clock tower sticking up in between, I might have imagined that I'd run all the way to a different city.

Horses clattered up and down the street, dragging behind them elaborate golden-and-black conveyances that looked nothing like Greta's simple cart. Even the humans here looked different from the ones in Greta's neighbourhood.

At least I'd learned some useful words during Greta's lecture that morning. The pale blue or yellow floor-length things worn by all of the female humans – no, *women* – were called 'dresses', and they looked enormously impractical, billowing out in massive circles around their owners' legs. The men wore 'trousers', which looked much more sensible, but Greta had been horrified that I was wearing them, as a girl. Still, at least mine were scale-coloured. Human trousers were so boring!

In dragon culture, bright colours were a source of pride, but human males seemed to be positively afraid of them. They might have been born with different-coloured skin, head-fur and eyes from each other, but they'd all chosen exactly the same type of plain, dark clothing, as if they were trying to blur together like herd animals. I hadn't glimpsed a single bright flash of crimson or gold since I'd arrived. Worse yet, for some reason the men around here seemed to be determined to half-strangle themselves with the elaborate white knots that they all had tied around their necks.

But none of the peculiarities that I saw before me mattered nearly as much as what I *smelt*.

There were food sellers on almost every street corner here, crying out the names of their wares over big, black, open ovens that stood smack in the centre of the pavement. Fresh, hot 'waffles' smelt sweet and sugary, and made me lick my lips. 'Jacket potatoes' sent up savoury scents, and 'roasted chestnuts' smelt strangely enticing. More scents drifted towards me from the open doorways up and down the street.

I was so hungry I would have whimpered if I'd had less dignity. It had been a very long time since my cheese and milk that morning … and apparently even tiny human stomachs needed more sustenance than that.

But there was something far more important than my hunger driving me now. It had been over a day since I'd tasted any chocolate!

Now that I'd finally found my passion, I wasn't going to stop until I had it in my claws forever.

Unfortunately, not a single one of the yellow-and-white buildings around me looked as if it could be made of chocolate. And with my weak new human nose, hunting out the smell of the city's famous chocolate houses underneath all those other scents that bombarded me – from the mouth-watering smells of the cooking food to the reek of human sweat, the strange artificial scents that the humans all seemed to slather on top of it and the steaming piles of droppings that the horses had left on the street ...

Well, it was going to be a challenge, even for a secret dragon.

But I was more than ready to try. I let go of the lamp-tree and set off to follow my nose, my cloth-covered feet squishing against the ground with every step.

CHAPTER 6

Chocolate houses were nothing like I'd expected.

When the scent of chocolate, growing stronger and stronger, led me to the open doorway of yet another yellow-and-white building, I stopped just outside it in disbelief.

Two humans nearly bumped into me from behind.

'Well, excuse me!' The woman, who was closer, yanked the edges of her big dress away from me, even though I hadn't touched it. Her bright red head-fur was piled on top of her head in bunches, and she had to tilt her pointy chin high to look down her wrinkled nose at me.

The man beside her cleared his throat, his dark skin flushing over his fancy neck-knot. 'If we might pass ...'

I gave them both a narrow-eyed, accusing glance. 'This building isn't made of chocolate!'

'Er ...' The man glanced at the woman beside him, the thin blocks of fur over his eyes shooting upward. 'No?' he said. But he didn't say it as if he was certain.

'Definitely not,' I assured him, and crossed my arms. 'So where can I find a real chocolate house in this city?'

At that, the woman's eyes rolled almost as alarmingly as Friedrich's had earlier that day. 'This *is* a real chocolate house, child,' she said. 'The most famous chocolate house in Drachenburg. I thought even country folk knew that!'

'We-e-ell ...' The man's shoulders moved up and down. 'I don't know if I'd say the *best*, Countess. The Chocolate Cup *is* the oldest and most established of the three chocolate houses, but Meckelhof's has become increasingly popular since the crown princess gave it her patronage, and I've even heard –'

'Nonsense! No one of any *real* importance favours Meckelhof's,' said the woman, 'and we needn't even *talk* about that little hole in the wall that calls itself a third chocolate house.' She sniffed. 'But regardless ...' Her brown gaze moved up and down, inspecting me from the top of my long black head-fur, which hung loose around my shoulders, to the mucky cloth coverings around my feet. 'The Chocolate Cup only caters to the very best society. So if you're looking for handouts, little girl, you'd be wise to look elsewhere.'

Handouts? I didn't know what that word meant, but I knew exactly how to read her look.

It was the same look my sister Citrine had given me during her last visit, when I'd told her that I didn't see the point in learning to write poetry in iambic pentameter. That look said, without the need for words: *You will never be impressive enough to be worthy of my attention.*

Unfortunately, I didn't have any fireballs to belch into this woman's face in answer. The look on Citrine's face when I had done *that* had been priceless.

Even without smoke or flame, though, I could roll my own eyes back at that countess, so I did, spinning them just as dizzily as any natural-born human might. Then I marched into the shop in front of her and firmly shut the door in her face.

Her outraged gasp reached me through the glass, but by then I hardly cared. The moment the shop door closed, I was knocked to my knees by the strength of the scent that rose to meet me.

Ohhh, chocolate!

It was even better than I'd remembered. Even better than the chocolate that the food mage had carried with him.

So rich. So intense. So pure.

So close!

I let out a little moan of yearning.

Dimly, I was aware that little black tables were scattered through the room before me, and that groups of humans were gathered in chattering groups around those tables. Even more vaguely, I was aware that the whole room seemed to be falling silent now, as all of them turned to stare at me where I knelt in front of the doorway.

None of it mattered. None of it was of the slightest interest to me compared to *that smell.*

Chocolate was scattered across all of the tables in various forms. Chocolate in bowls. Chocolate in glasses. There were even more chocolatey delicacies sitting in vast glittering glass cases to my left. But I wanted the real thing: the *source*.

I rose to my feet and aimed myself at the open door at the back of the room as if I was being yanked by a wonderful, invisible chain.

'I *beg* your pardon!' A black-clad human with skin as pale as chalk lunged forward to stand in my path before I'd made it two full steps. 'Do you have a reservation, miss?'

'A *what*?' I batted at him, but he didn't move out of my way, and he was too solid for me to slip around him.

'The Chocolate Cup is far too busy to welcome any customers without prior reservations.' His thin lips curled as he gazed down at me. 'So, if you don't have a reservation, as I strongly assume from both your clothing *and* your manners ... !'

A titter of laughter sounded from the nearby tables.

I shook my head impatiently. Why was he wasting my time with this nonsense?

'I'm not a *customer*, whatever that is,' I said. 'I'm your new apprentice.'

He blinked three times, quickly, his lips uncurling. '*Our* apprentice?'

'Absolutely,' I said. 'I've come here to work.' I might not know much about human society, but I'd figured out apprenticeships by now, from the hints that Greta had let drop on our journey: an apprentice was someone who learned how to work with things. And what else in the world would I ever want to work with?

Jasper had his philosophy, Citrine had her poetry and, at long last, I had chocolate. Now that that heavenly scent finally surrounded me, it was almost enough to make me stop aching for my wings and claws.

But then he ruined it.

'You?' he said. He looked me up and down and then burst into laughter. '*You?*'

I frowned at him, shaking my long, tangled black head-fur out of my face to meet his eyes directly. 'Of course *me*,' I said. 'Who else would I be talking about?'

But he didn't answer. He was laughing too hard. The whole shopful of humans was laughing with him, too.

And they kept on laughing as he picked me up by both arms and carried me out of the shop a moment later.

It didn't matter how much I struggled, or how hard I kicked his legs along the way with my slippery, muck-and-cloth-covered feet. There was no way to make him drop me until we were three full feet away from the shop windows. Then, finally, he lifted his hands and let me go.

Ouch!

I landed hard on my backside in the middle of the dirty, bumpy stone street. Horses whinnied behind me and a human cursed me for getting in his way. Something terrible squished underneath my out-flung hands.

The chocolate-house guard wiped his own hands together and strode back into the building, ignoring the chaos in the street outside.

Well, he wouldn't ignore me for long! I jumped up and lunged for the doorway ...

Just as he closed the door in my face. A hard metallic click sounded on the other side. When I tried the handle, it wouldn't move, no matter how furiously I yanked at it.

As I peered through the immovable glass door of the Chocolate Cup, I saw every human inside rise to their feet, smacking their hands together in applause for the chocolate guard.

He bent forward with an elaborate flourish, and the applause grew even louder. That countess I'd closed the door on earlier was clapping hardest of all.

I glared at those smug, puny humans through the glass and set my teeth together with a snap.

They thought they'd got rid of me, did they? Well, this wasn't the only chocolate house in Drachenburg. According to the snooty countess's friend, it might not even be the best.

There were two more chocolate houses in this city. All I had to do was find them.

Finding the second chocolate house wasn't a problem. It turned out to be only two streets away, in a yellow-and-white shop that could have been a twin to the Chocolate Cup.

Unfortunately, it had a guard, too. This one was a woman, but she was just as strong as the first guard. After tossing me out of her own chocolate house, she lingered outside to give me a lecture, ticking off her points on her dark brown fingers as I lay on the street before her.

'Firstly, *everyone* wants to work with chocolate, ever since the first chocolatier from Villenne set up shop in Drachenburg five years ago. Here at Meckelhof's, we're honoured to have the crown princess's own patronage, so we only take the very best of the best apprentices, and then only with a proper reference ... which you –' she swept me with a clear, calm gaze – 'clearly don't possess.

'Secondly, you're dressed like a beggar and you stink of the streets, so no reputable shop would ever take you seriously as an apprentice chocolatier, even if you did have a reference. Making chocolate is an art, not a craft, so chocolatiers can only come from the respectable classes.

'Thirdly, you clearly have no manners, so you couldn't be a waitress and serve our customers their chocolate even if we gave you new clothes for the job.

'And fourthly –' she shook her head as she looked down at me, her expression infuriatingly compassionate – 'why don't you visit the public baths? If you clean yourself up, then perhaps, if you're really lucky, someone may take you on as a maid.'

Oh, I would have eaten her for that if I could. I would have devoured her in an instant. I would have sent her up in flames!

But only a pitiful, toothless snarl came out of my small, human mouth, and she didn't even seem to hear it as she turned away, tossing her final advice over her shoulder.

'There's no point wanting what you can't have, little girl ... and chocolate isn't for the likes of you.'

Then she walked back into the chocolate house where

she reigned and didn't even bother to close the door behind her.

Seething, I lay in the street and absorbed my new information, as horses trotted around me and human curses floated over my head.

What was the point of being human if I couldn't be around chocolate? I'd finally found the thing I wanted to work with for the rest of my life, but no one here would even let me near it. If only I had my wings and claws! Then I could go ahead and just *take* it, like a proper dragon, whether they liked it or not.

If I ever saw that dastardly food mage again, I would *bite* him! I didn't care if my human teeth were too blunt and puny to do real damage.

I would make him take back his spell, no matter what it took. And then ...

I pushed myself up on to my hands and knees and stepped on to the pavement, gritting my teeth in determination.

Dragons never gave up! And there was still one more chocolate house in Drachenburg, even if that snooty countess had called it a hole in the wall not worth talking about.

I'd grown up in a cavern. I *liked* holes in the wall.

And even if, by human standards, I didn't look 'respectable' enough to work with chocolate ... well, why on earth should I let that stop me? I'd been through one transformation already in the last two days.

Now, apparently, it was time for a second.

How hard could it be?

CHAPTER 7

I'd had no idea that human beings cared so much about money.

None of Jasper's philosophers respected it, as I knew from bitter experience. A year ago, when I had beaten him in a competition to see how many human crowns and necklaces we could each fit around our claws, my brother had sulked for an hour and a half and then bored me senseless with quotes from a loooooong human book about how meaningless gold and jewels really were.

The shopkeepers in Drachenburg wouldn't have taken any more notice of that high-minded philosophy than I had myself, when I'd waved my triumphantly glittering claws in Jasper's face. They probably would have thrown the author of that book out of their shops if he'd ever tried to quote himself at them.

Humans, it turned out, didn't give anything away for free.

It wasn't until I'd been tramping around Drachenburg for hours, with my stomach growling and my feet hurting worse than ever, that I finally found something I could sell in return.

'Hey!' a human girl called out behind me, as I stomped away from yet another useless dress shop. 'Wait up!' She grabbed my arm and pulled me around to face her with a cocky grin, like a predator who was sure of her prey. She looked about the same age as me, but she was at least a hand's height taller, and she carried herself with so much swagger and confidence she seemed decades older.

But that didn't mean she was going to get the better of me. I yanked myself free, growling, 'What do you want? I left your stupid shop, didn't I?'

'Oh, I don't work for them,' she said. 'Do I *look* like a fashionable dressmaker's apprentice?' She waved one hand impatiently at her dark green, masculine trousers and coat, which hung off her tall, skinny body as if they'd been made for someone else, and waved her other hand at her black head-fur, which stood out around her dark brown face in tight, wiry curls, shorter than any other female head-fur I'd seen all day. 'I've been watching you for the past half hour, going in and out of all the dressmakers' shops. You need new clothes now that you're in the big city, don't you? But you don't have enough money to buy any.'

I didn't trust helpful-seeming humans at all. I gave this one a haughty look, raising the face-fur over my eyes just as I'd seen other humans do. 'So?'

'So, I know somewhere else you can go.' Her own face-fur furrowed as she frowned down at me, pursing her lips. If I looked twelve, she couldn't have been more than thirteen at the absolute oldest – and she was definitely human – but the expression on her face just then made her look disconcertingly like my mother. 'It all depends on how much you care about your hair.'

'My *what*?' I blinked at her.

'You know. Hair? This stuff?' She reached out and yanked my long, straight head-fur. 'Are you attached to it?'

My head swam as I stared at her, trying to make sense of her words. As I had already learned, humans and logic didn't seem to exist in the same universe.

'How could I not be attached to my hair?' I asked. 'It wouldn't stay on otherwise!'

'Ha!' She snorted, her dark eyes gleaming. 'Come on.' She took a firm hold of my arm, and this time, reluctantly, I let her, as she told me, 'I'm Silke, and I'll show you exactly where to go.'

Of all the things that humans bought and sold, their own hair had to be the strangest. But for some reason long head-fur like mine held real value to them. So I sat very still, without growling or biting, on a tall seat in a tiny shop in a neighbourhood where the skinny, crumbling grey buildings were pressed tightly together and the dull colours on the shop walls were visibly peeling away. Silke stood to one side of my chair, watching with her arms crossed and her gaze intent while the owner of the shop chopped off my hair in thick hanks until the remaining bits barely reached my ears.

'There!' Silke said. 'That's thirty marks' worth at least.'

The hair-chopper, a grim old man without a neck-knot, harrumphed. 'Twenty, maybe, if –'

'Twenty-five,' said Silke, and held out her hand, wiggling her fingers impatiently.

Sighing, he reached into his pocket and dropped a small pile of coins on to her palm.

I watched, narrow-eyed, as they clinked together. 'Shouldn't I be the one who gets those?'

'Of course,' said my helper, and flashed me a smile. 'All but my commission.'

Her 'commission', apparently, was one large silver coin, which she slipped out of my pile and into a pouch that had been cleverly hidden inside her loose coat. I glared after it as I closed my fingers around the other silver and copper coins she'd handed me. 'How many marks do I have left?'

'That's twenty,' Silke said, and pushed open the front door of the shop. 'Luckily, I know exactly where you can find a perfect dress, already made up, for that price. And it's nearly new, too!'

Grandfather always said there were times when you had to ride the wind currents and see where they took you, when food was scarce and you didn't know where the prey was hiding. So I followed her out of the shop without complaint.

My brain hadn't stopped working, though. As she led me through the crowds, weaving her way with easy confidence, I memorised every street turning and landmark. I would be able to find my way back even in the dark. And I might be small in human form, but I was still the fiercest creature in this city.

All the same, my stomach sank when I saw the dress that Silke had picked out for me. 'You're not serious?'

We were in something that Silke called a 'market' by then, nearly half an hour's walk from where we'd left most of my hair. Unlike the snooty yellow-and-white shops of central Drachenburg, with their identically painted walls and glass doors, the market was an outdoor scrabble of cloth dens and rickety wooden tables, all huddled along the muddy bank of a long brown river. Goods were spread out for sale on those tables … And the dress that Silke held up so proudly was nearly as muddy-looking as the river itself.

'What's wrong with it?' Silke demanded. She traced one finger lovingly over its dark brown folds. 'No stains, no rips and it's only last year's fashion. It –'

'I need to look respectable!' I said. 'That one's just … boring.'

Silke rolled her eyes. 'Respectable *is* boring,' she said. 'Haven't you learned that yet?'

By that time, human eye-rolling didn't even startle me. I crossed my arms and jutted my chin out at her, making myself bigger in the human way. 'I can't wear that,' I told her firmly. 'I need to cover myself in colour.' No dragon in the world would take me seriously if I wore plain, unornamented brown. I wanted to roar my declaration of power to everyone who saw me, not hide like a frightened herd animal trying to blend in with her surroundings.

'Oh, fine.' Silke sighed heavily. 'But I think you're making a big mistake.'

'Do you?' I looked pointedly between her and the older brown-skinned male human – not yet a man – who ran the little cloth den where Silke had found the dress. I was getting better and better at spotting the differences between humans ... and their similarities, too. 'Do you know what I think? I think that this place belongs to your family and you're trying to trick me into giving *all* my money to you.'

Silke's eyes widened as she flashed a sidelong glance at the male human, who was serving another customer in a series of movements just as quick and graceful as Silke's own. Then she began to laugh, giving me a surprisingly different-looking smile than I'd seen from her all afternoon. 'You're not as simple as you seem, are you, country girl?'

'My name,' I told her, 'is Aventurine.'

'*Definitely* not from around here.' Silke's smile widened. 'Well, I wouldn't worry too much about that. People here come from all over the world. Even our late queen came all the way from across the sea when she married our king, years ago. Once your family's been here for a generation, you'll turn into a local just like me, and like our crown princess, too.'

She gave me a firm nod. 'So, *Aventurine*, here's the

truth. This is a good-quality dress, and I can even make it two marks cheaper, as a personal favour. But I can't help you out at any of the other stalls around here, because none of them belongs to my family.'

'Hmm,' I said sceptically. I turned to look at the other dens and tables that surrounded us on the riverbank. 'I think I'd better find out first how much the other dresses cost, before I trust that yours is any cheaper.'

'You're learning fast.' Silke sighed, but I didn't miss the reluctant admiration in her voice. When she'd thought I was easy prey, she hadn't liked me. Now that I was finally showing my teeth, she did.

The truth was, I liked her, too. I liked the way she broke the human rules of behaviour by wearing male clothing, and I liked her strength and determination, even if she had tried to use them to trick me. She might be a human, but there was definitely a touch of dragon to her. Dragons fought fiercely for their families, too. It would have been fun to play-fight with her if we'd been properly armed with teeth and claws.

As it was, I gave her a smile that bared my teeth – the closest I could come to flaring my wings and showing off all my scales. 'I'll see you later then,' I told her. 'If I don't find a cheaper dress at another stall.'

'Fine,' Silke said. Her eyes narrowed. 'But remember, you're still awfully new here, and it isn't easy to be a girl alone in this city. You could use a friend to help you get on.'

For a moment, as I looked at the cocky, dragon-ish tilt of her head, I was actually tempted.

Then I caught myself, just in time. *Never trust a human!* If I'd ever needed proof of Grandfather's rule, Greta had given me plenty that afternoon. Where would I be right now if I'd been stupid enough to trust the first humans who'd brought me into town?

I remembered Greta's sickly-sweet voice cooing into my ears as her fingers pinched into my shoulder ... and I bit back a snarl as I turned and walked away, leaving Silke safely behind me.

Dragons didn't need human friends.

And I'd been right: the other stalls were cheaper.

Twenty minutes later I was wearing a bright gold-and-purple dress that only belled out a few reasonable inches around my feet. I'd had to roll up the sleeves to keep them from falling over my fingers and getting in my way, but the dress had cost only ten marks, and for an extra five I had a new pair of bright red shoes to protect my feet, too. Better yet, I'd cleaned my hands and face with a nice damp cloth, and I still had one shiny silver coin left for later. I wrapped it up inside the long silver-and-crimson folds of my first outfit and tucked the whole thing under my arm.

The stall owner who'd sold me the dress and shoes gave me a thoughtful look as I turned to leave. 'You know ... if you'd like another couple of marks, I wouldn't mind taking that funny red-and-silver thing off your hands, so you don't have to carry it with you. No one would ever want to wear it, of course, but it's a nice enough pattern that we could probably rip it up and use it for scrap fabric.'

Rip it up? My arm tightened around the thick wad. It was all that was left of my beautiful silver-and-crimson scales!

Each brightly coloured piece of the pattern on the cloth was marked by a careful curving line that showed exactly where each of my scales had been imprinted. Even my old spikes were there, forming a line of tiny silver hooks along the back that sealed the outfit when I wore it. As I looked down at it now, my raw, vulnerable human skin prickled in a wave of hot shivers that raced all the way from my toes to the nape of my neck. Sudden thunder drummed in my ears. It was the echo of every frantic roar that had been bottled up in my chest ever since my transformation.

Those were *my scales* on that cloth.

And this human wanted to *destroy them*?

'*Never!*' I snarled.

I spun around, holding the last pieces of my past against my chest, and marched off in search of my future.

THE CHOCOLATE
HEART

CHAPTER 8

My stomach growled ferociously as I strode through the narrow, crowded streets of outer Drachenburg. I ignored its complaints, just as I ignored the stabbing pains in my scraped and blistered feet and the aches in my puny human leg muscles. The smell of freshly cooking sausages rose from the open oven of a street vendor and twined around me in savoury temptation as I passed, but I braced myself against it and breathed through my mouth, doing my best to shut off all the sensations from my nose. Another stall owner with an outdoor oven, a street further on, was selling a strange twisted form of bread he called 'pretzels', that I could have devoured in a heartbeat, but I forced myself past with barely a hitch in my stride. When I passed a waffle oven two minutes later, I didn't even let out the snarl of desperation that wanted to rip itself from my throat.

If all I had was five marks, I would not waste them. I was a fierce, powerful dragon despite my current body problems, and I *could* control myself, no matter what Mother or Jasper thought.

I just wished that all the horses I passed didn't look so delicious.

By the time I reached the broader, brighter streets around the first two chocolate houses, I was breathing hard from the effort of holding myself back. My teeth were gritted – the better to keep myself from lunging into the street and *biting* – and strange beads of moisture kept popping up on my forehead and neck. When three humans in a row veered out of my way, though, looking visibly worried, I forced myself to stop and take a deep breath.

Respectable. I was supposed to look respectable, not frightening. Even the most open-minded chocolatier wouldn't hire an apprentice who looked ready to eat everyone around them – even if that was the literal truth.

I can do this. I threw back my shoulders and plastered a wide, human smile on my face.

There was only one problem, as I realised a few minutes later: the third chocolate house was nowhere to be found. Beyond all the yellow-and-white shops that I'd walked past before, I found streets of ornamented grand houses with high, spiked gates like dragon's teeth, and I caught sight of an even grander palace in the distance ... but I couldn't have cared less about any of that nonsense.

I finally gave up and asked for directions.

'You're looking for a chocolate house?' The man I'd stopped looked harried and distracted, his eyes already moving past me towards some final destination. 'The Chocolate Cup is –'

'No!' I said. I couldn't hide the impatience in my tone, but I stretched my lips even further into my most impressive smile to make up for it. 'Not the Chocolate Cup *or* Meckelhof's. I want the third chocolate shop. The hole in the wall.'

'The – oh. *Oh!*' His gaze finally moved to my face, and he blinked, taking a quick step backwards and tugging nervously on his neck-knot.

Oops. Maybe I was showing a few too many teeth in my smile. I relaxed my face muscles, and saw his shoulders sag in response.

'I know which one you mean,' he said, 'although I haven't been there myself, obviously.'

Obviously? I stood in silence, holding him in my unblinking gaze as I waited for him to say something useful.

The face-fur over his eyes lowered, making him look oddly nervous again. His words sped up as his eyes fixed on mine. 'It's not in the first district, you see. It's about fifteen minutes' walk from here, in the third district, where the jumped-up merchants and the bankers live. No one I know would ever go there.'

I didn't move or even blink. I was still waiting for the information that I'd asked for.

He swallowed visibly. 'Your eyes ... you know, their colour, um, it's very unusual. I'm not sure I've ever seen it in a human be– I mean ...' He tugged even harder on his neck-knot, his face turning pinker and pinker.

'Oh, for heaven's sake!' Silke suddenly slipped into place beside me, appearing seemingly out of nowhere and heaving a dramatic sigh. 'I give up. This is too painful to witness!' She waved one dismissive hand at my informant. 'Don't worry, sir, I'll take her where she wants to go. You're free!'

'What?' I swung around to stare at her. 'What are you doing here?' I demanded. 'I don't need your help, remember?'

'Oh, I didn't come to *help* you,' Silke said, as the other human backed warily away from us both. 'I followed because I was curious, obviously. I wasn't planning to even let you see me! But if you don't leave this poor man alone soon, he's going to faint from sheer panic, so I'm taking over out of pity.' She grasped my arm. 'Trust me, *no one* knows this city like I do. You're looking for the third district, right?'

'That depends.' I braced myself, planting my feet firmly on the pavement. 'What are you going to ask for in payment?'

She chuckled. 'No more than you can afford, country girl. This time I'm just looking for information.'

I narrowed my eyes at her suspiciously, then shrugged. 'Fine.' I fell into step beside her, turning away from the useless male human without regret.

A whooshing sigh of relief sounded behind us as we left. *Humans!* It was as if no one had ever asked him a simple question before.

I would never understand this species.

'So,' Silke said brightly, as she led me back on to a busy shopping street, 'what business do you have at that chocolate house you're looking for? Because you know no one like us would ever be allowed inside.'

We'll see about that. I stayed silent, firmly closing my lips.

'No answers, eh?' She gave me a mischievous grin. 'All right, I don't mind making up my own stories to explain it. How about ... your family had to sneak out of Drachenburg fifty years ago to escape their enemies, but before they left they buried half of their fabulous treasure in a secret hiding place under that shop. Now you're going back to sneak it out again and become a rich girl with a dozen servants! Am I right?'

'What kind of fool would ever leave treasure behind them?' I shook my head at her in disgust. 'That doesn't make any sense.' Even humans wouldn't be stupid enough to abandon their own hoards ... would they?

'Not that, then.' Silke sounded pleased. 'Hmm, let's see ...' She led me swiftly down the street, weaving gracefully through the bustling crowd. 'In that case, maybe you're actually a noblewoman in disguise, and –'

'Don't you have anything better to do than make up stories about me?' I asked. 'More clothes to sell to country girls, maybe?'

'Oh, I don't spend all day selling clothes,' said Silke. 'That's my brother's job. Dieter *likes* sitting in one place. I prefer to keep on my feet and see what happens in my city. And *you're* the most interesting thing that's happened here in a while.'

She hummed to herself, rocking back and forth on her boot heels as we waited at a street corner for a tangle of carriages to pass. The horses neighed at each other in fury, and the people shouted in angry counterpoint, but a dangerous-looking smile spread across Silke's face. 'I know. Maybe you're the first human ever to escape from the fairies' underground kingdom in Elfenwald, and *that's* why you don't know how anything works in the normal world!'

'*What?*' The knot of carriages finally parted, but I didn't move. My mouth dropped open as I glared at my guide, torn between disbelief and smoking outrage. 'You think I'd ever have anything to do with *fairies?*'

Of course dragons were wary of humans, but we absolutely *despised* fairies. They might not have been spotted above ground in over a hundred years, but my family still told stories about how infuriating they were.

Only a few, dangerous humans could use magic, but fairies had so much of it, it glowed out of their skin like internal fire ... and they were determined to cause mischief, especially for dragons. The only good thing about them, Grandfather always said, was that now that they'd all gone into hiding underground, we didn't have to eat them to get rid of them any more.

Apparently, they tasted terrible.

But Silke laughed, a bright peal of delight, as she looked at my outraged face. 'Well, well. *That* finally got your attention, didn't it?' She tugged my arm, pulling me towards the street. 'If you really want to stop people wondering where you come from, by the way, you might want to think about changing more than your clothes. Who's ever heard of a girl named *Aventurine*?' She shook her head, a glint of mischief in her eyes. 'I know. How about we call you *Eva*? That's a nice ordinary name, with no mysteries at all. Just the way you like it, right?'

'Argh!' Gritting my teeth, I pulled my arm free and stomped across the street, turning the next corner at Silke's direction ... then rocked to a sudden halt as my nose picked up an amazing scent.

There!

'The third district,' Silke said cheerfully. 'We aren't far now!'

The identical yellow-and-white buildings of the first district were gone, replaced by houses of every colour. Skinny pink buildings stood pressed against bright blue, yellow or green ones, all rising high into the sky, with shops spilling out of their bottom floors on to the pavements outside. The chocolate smell was coming from only a few doors away, tugging at me like a delicious promise.

I didn't see any chocolate, though, only humans, dressed every bit as ridiculously here as they had been in the first district. If anything, the men's neck-knots were even more elaborate, and the women's skirts billowed even wider.

And all of the women in dresses had long hair. Why hadn't I noticed that part before? I'd been trying so hard to make myself look respectable with my new clothes, but had I ruined everything by letting my hair be cut?

Something very strange happened inside me as I looked from one long-haired woman to another in the street around me. It was as if my chest was growing smaller and tighter with every step. I could barely fit my breath through it any more. Worse still, something was pulsing hard and fast against my throat, as if a tiny bird had got trapped there and was trying to batter its way out.

'The chocolate house is just up ahead,' Silke told me. 'Come on, mysterious Aventurine-from-nowhere. They'll never let us in to join their fancy customers, but you might as well take a peek through their windows now that we've come all this way.'

Never let us in.

My feet wouldn't shift when I tried to lift them.

What was happening to my new body?

I rubbed one hand against my chest, trying to loosen it back to normal. But my tiny new heart beat so rapidly against my hand, I knew immediately that something had gone horribly wrong with it.

Did human hearts often go wrong for no reason? What would happen if mine exploded inside me now, as I stood only a few doors down from the source of that delicious chocolate smell? I'd never eat any chocolate again! But then, I might never taste chocolate again anyway if the guard at this chocolate house took one look at my too-short hair and turned me away without a second thought. Then I'd have nowhere to go, and no chocolate, ever, and ...

Whooosh!

I staggered and fell forward. Clamping my hands around my knees, I fought to draw a full breath.

'Aventurine? What's wrong?' Silke's voice sounded far away – miles from my malfunctioning body.

No, no, no, this cannot be happening!

I would *not* let my new body fail me. Not now! I was only a few doors away from all my hopes for the future. Of all the times in my life when I had to be healthy and strong, now was the single most important moment. I had to look and act like a normal, respectable human. I had to –

'*And stay out!*' bellowed a female voice three doors ahead of me.

My head shot up. A tall, pale-skinned boy had just come hurtling out of that doorway that smelt of heaven. My stomach sank as I took in the sight of him.

From his elaborate neck-knot to his boring dark trousers, he was the most respectable-looking human I'd seen all day. And they'd still thrown him out on to the street?

I *don't have a chance.*

But no. This boy had run outside himself, and now he spun back around to shake his fist at the doorway. 'I'd never come back even if you begged me! You're the most unreasonable chocolatier in this entire city. You don't care about anything except your stupid rules, and –'

'And *you* know nothing of good chocolate!' the voice bellowed back. 'I should never have hired you. All you care about are appearances, not quality!'

'Ha!' The boy jerked his chin up as he smoothed down his green coat. 'It's no wonder no one important ever comes here, with an attitude like that. You'll be closed down within half a year if you're lucky. Less than that, when I tell my uncle how you – aaargh!' He ducked as something came flying through the air after him.

'I won't forget this!' he yelled as he turned away, protecting his head with both arms. 'And neither will my family! No one respectable will come anywhere near you or your stupid hole-in-the-wall shop ever again!'

A wordless roar of rage billowed out of the doorway and followed after him as he ran away and disappeared around the corner.

'Phew.' Silke let out a low whistle. 'Maybe we should wait a minute or two before we look through those windows, eh? Or try a different chocolate house?'

'Are you joking?' I shook my head as I straightened. My heartbeat had slowed down again. I could breathe. And my chest felt just fine. In fact, I felt *excellent*. 'This is absolutely perfect!'

I might not know what had caused my human body to go wild for a few minutes, but I knew exactly the sort of sound that had just come from inside that shop. And I couldn't wait to meet whoever had just made it.

'You're delirious.' Silke stared at me. 'No wonder you almost fainted. Why don't I take you back to the market now? We can find you some food, talk about where you really come from, and –'

'No.' I unfolded my scale-cloth and pulled out the single silver coin that I had left. 'Thank you for your help,' I told her, holding out the money. 'Maybe I *will* see you again sometime after all.'

'I can't take that!' She held her hands flat in front of her, looking horrified, as she backed away from my outstretched hand. 'It's all you have left, remember? And anyway, it's too much. All I did was show you the way to a wild woman's chocolate house!'

For the first time ever, I touched a human on purpose, folding Silke's long brown fingers securely over the coin. 'Trust me,' I told her. 'That's exactly what I was looking for.'

The closer I came to the open front door, the more incredible it smelt.

The Chocolate Heart, read the sign over the entrance. Once I'd said goodbye to Silke, I had to use my bony human elbows to force my way past all the other whispering onlookers, but I ignored their complaints and glowering looks. After all, none of them seemed to want to go into the shop, despite the delectable smells wafting out from it. So it only made sense for them to make way for serious visitors.

Not that there were many in the Chocolate Heart itself. As I stepped through the front door, breathing in the incredible scent of pure chocolate, I saw empty table after empty table in the small, flame-coloured front room. The only customers I spotted were sitting clustered around three gold-coloured tables near the back, watching with obvious horror as two humans argued in the centre of the room, their arms waving wildly and their voices rising louder and louder with every word.

The taller one, a man with dark brown skin who looked as if he was in physical pain, said, 'You can't just go around behaving like –'

'He was poisoning my chocolate!' bellowed the woman. She was short and stocky and golden-skinned, and I recognised her voice immediately. 'He should never have been allowed in my kitchen in the first place!'

'He was *not* poisoning the chocolate!' The man spun around to wave frantically at the remaining customers, two of whom had already got to their feet and started to sidle nervously towards the door. 'That was only a figure of speech. Please do not pass it on! You know what a perfectionist our great chocolatier is. She only means –'

'He *was* poisoning it!' snarled the woman. 'What else would you call it, when he was deliberately ruining the flavour of my chocolate by using substandard ingredients? He was too lazy to grate the fresh nutmeg, so –'

'He is the lord mayor's *nephew*,' said the man. He clenched his fingers in his short wiry hair and tugged at it in what looked like desperation. 'Not everything is about chocolate! Can't you understand that?'

'Ha!' The woman snorted and crossed her big arms. 'Maybe in those fancy first-district shops it's not, but in *my* chocolate house –'

'Even if you had to dismiss him, could you not have just *tried* to be polite, for once in your life?' the man demanded, as the remaining customers sneaked past me out of the front door. 'Couldn't you have recommended him to a chef at one of the local restaurants to get rid of him without insult? Or –'

'He should feel lucky I didn't toss him into my oven!' the woman roared, as the final few customers fled the shop. She spun around and pointed one accusing finger at the doorway where I stood. 'I can tell you right now, if he ever dares show his face here again ...' She halted, her own face crunching into a furious scowl as her gaze finally landed on me. 'And what are *you* looking at?'

What was I looking at? For the first time since my transformation, my human lips stretched into a sincere smile all on their own.

The smell of heavenly chocolate rose all around me. The walls blazed with colour, a gorgeous, hot blend of orange and crimson. The woman before me had a roar that would have made any dragon proud. And I'd just found a chocolate house that really was all about the chocolate.

'I'm your new apprentice,' I told her.

I knew exactly what I was looking at: my new home.

CHAPTER 9

'Ha!' said the woman again, and flung both her arms into the air. Turning sharply, she marched towards the pair of doors at the back of the room. 'Apprentices – pah! I've had enough of them.'

The man closed his eyes for a moment as she passed him, lines popping up all over his forehead. Then he sighed and looked at me. 'Ah ...' His weary gaze travelled from my short spiky dark hair to the red toes of my shoes, peeping out from underneath my new purple-and-gold dress. 'We will be looking for a new apprentice, it is true, but I'm afraid right now isn't ideal timing, and –'

'I'll grate all the nutmeg!' I said. *Whatever that is.* 'I won't skip any steps or use any substandard ingredients, ever. I'll do anything you tell me to, to make the chocolate better. That's all I want – to learn how to make the best chocolate ever.'

The woman paused, turning back to look at me with one hand already resting on the door in front of her. 'The best chocolate ever, eh?' The face-fur over her eyes lowered as she studied me, her dark eyes piercing.

'Chocolate is my passion,' I told her.

'Oh, for ... !' The man let out a pained half-laugh and shook his head. 'We appreciate your enthusiasm, young lady, but may I ask: do you have any actual references? Any chefs who can vouch for your talents? Or any connections to important civic leaders or members of this community?'

'No.' My chest was starting to tighten again, my breath growing shorter, as I felt all of my lovely warm certainty start to slide away from me. 'But ... it's all about the chocolate here, isn't it?'

There was a moment of silence as the man and woman looked at each other.

I clenched my hands around my folded-up scale-cloth and forced myself to stay silent as they argued without words.

Finally, the man let out a hissing breath through his teeth. 'Yes,' he said tightly, 'of course the chocolate is the most important part. But still – does your family have any influence at all? Any connections that might help our shop?'

They both turned their heads towards me, waiting for my answer.

I swallowed hard, conscious of Silke standing outside

the window with the rest of the crowd, watching everything that happened inside with intense curiosity.

At least she wouldn't be surprised. She'd told me that I would never be allowed to stay inside a place like this.

'No,' I said numbly. 'No connections at all. Just – chocolate.'

'Right.' He sighed and shook his head. 'In that case –'

'Quite,' the woman said briskly. 'I think we're finished here, don't you?' She pushed against the two back doors with both hands, and they swung wide open, emitting a burst of scent that made my mouth water. 'Well?' she demanded. 'Are you coming or not, girl?'

My mouth dropped open. So did the man's, as he swivelled around to stare at her. 'Now, wait one minute, Marina ...'

'I'm coming!' I said, and hurried after the chocolatier before she could change her mind.

'Think of it this way, Horst.' Marina tossed the words back over her shoulder. 'If this girl hasn't got any fancy connections, then no one important will be offended when I toss *her* out on her ear for being useless. That should make you happy!'

He only let out a groan in reply.

But I didn't have any time to worry about the future. I needed every bit of my attention right now for the cavern full of chocolatey bliss lying before me.

There were enough jewel colours in Marina's kitchen to make any dragon hum with pleasure. The clean white walls were lined with shelves of tall, curving pots made of glinting silver, copper and gold, along with stacks of blue-and-white porcelain cups with intricately curling and orna-mented handles. If I'd been back home in my cavern, I would have spent hours running my claws around every one of them, inspecting them with pure delight.

But they weren't the best part of the kitchen. Not by a long way.

Where the front room had been painted the colours of fire, this room was full of flames, smoke and heat that didn't have to be imagined. A big white oven bulked in front of me with a long piece of heavy stone laid on top of one of its grates. On my right, a long charcoal brazier billowed more smoke into the room, while two copper kettles and a massive silver-coloured pot cooked above it. On my left, a giant fireplace filled one full wall of the room, sending out so much heat I could have basked in front of it for hours.

A funny gold-coloured metal contraption hung over the hot fire, suspended on a long, thin bar, smoking with heat and turning over and over again without any human hand touching it. With each new turn, a shower of rattles erupted inside the metal casing, as if a whole pile of small, hard pebbles was being roasted inside it ... but as I breathed in deeply my nose assured me that whatever was hidden within was much, much more intriguing than mere pebbles.

And then the smell from the kettles and the metal pot and – !

So many scents washed over me at once that I staggered, my vision blurring.

'Watch out!' Marina said sharply.

I yanked myself upright just before I could stumble into the table beside me. It was covered by more than a dozen glasses with long, thin stems leading up to curving, shallow bowls, each of them filled with a dark, creamy-looking substance that smelt amazing.

If she hadn't stopped me, I would have knocked at least half of them off the table.

I gritted my teeth and refused to apologise.

'Where shall I start?' I asked, jerking my chin up and walking further into the room.

She didn't follow me. 'When was the last time you ate?'

'Who, me?' I blinked at her. 'This morning.' I frowned, thinking back. '*Early* morning.'

'I might have known.' She let out a hiss through her teeth. 'Of all the absurd –'

'I don't need food,' I told her. 'I need work.'

'And how are you going to do any work for me if you're swooning all over the place, ninny?'

I only understood about half of what she'd just said to me, but it was more than enough to make my face-fur draw together into a frown. 'My name's not "ninny".'

'I don't care what your name is. You're not setting to work in *my* kitchen without food in your belly. Hunger leads to distraction, which leads to carelessness – and you'd better learn right now that I don't tolerate carelessness in my chocolate house, not now, not ever. So ...' She scooped up one of the glasses full of sweet-smelling darkness and handed it to me along with a long silver spoon. 'Here. The people who ordered these ran away like frightened bunnies five minutes ago. You might as well eat one instead of letting them all go to waste.'

Dragons could go for days without food when they needed to, and I didn't like being treated as if I was weak. Still, as the scent drifted up from the glass in my hands, I lost the will to argue. 'Fine,' I muttered, and dug in.

The first taste made my head spin all over again. The second taste made pleasure shoot up and down my body in a shower of gold.

A moment later I stared down at the empty glass in my hands, almost moaning when I realised I was finished. 'What *was* that?'

Marina looked at me with her face-fur raised and her arms crossed. 'You tell me,' she said. 'What did it taste like?'

I closed my eyes, running my tongue along the top of my mouth and trying to soak in any last tendrils of taste. 'Well, obviously there was chocolate –' *so* rich, so silky, so intense, my stomach felt warm at the thought of it – 'and then there must have been milk of some sort – no, thick cream ...' I'd tasted them both on that cart ride, so I knew the difference.

'And then ... oh, there was definitely cinnamon.' Nothing could make me forget that flavour! 'And something else to make it taste so sweet. But there were at least two other spices in it for flavour, and I don't know either of their names.' I opened my eyes and met her gaze, refusing to lower my own or look ashamed. 'I don't know the names of a lot of things here, yet.'

She studied me for a long moment. Then she nodded. 'Fair enough. The other two spices were nutmeg and vanilla. You'll learn the taste of them fast enough if you work in this kitchen, I can promise you that.'

Nutmeg and *vanilla.* I memorised the names, filing them away.

'Now,' she said, 'I want you to taste this.' She strode to the charcoal brazier on my right and unhooked one of the copper kettles from the closest grate. 'Pass me one of those chocolate pots, will you?'

Following her pointing finger, I stood up on my toes and lifted down one of the lovely silver pots from the shelf nearby. It looked almost like a kettle, but it had two lids instead of one and it was far too dainty to survive a fiery stovetop. If I hadn't been so curious about what was coming next, I would have taken a moment to play with the different lids and work it out like a puzzle. Instead I handed it to Marina before she could ask a second time.

'Good.' She opened the lower lid and poured in the contents of the kettle. Dark, rich brown liquid streamed through the air, sending up a cloud of steam that made me close my eyes for a moment as I breathed it in.

Hot chocolate. Oh, this was definitely hot chocolate – but not like the food mage had made it. Not at all.

Incredibly, it smelt even better. Richer. More intense. And there was something else about it, something ...

I'd moved closer without even realising it.

'Watch out!' She nudged me back with one strong arm as she reached towards the closest table. 'Now it's time for the molinet.' She picked up a long wooden tool with a wide, ridged bottom, and flipped open the top lid of the chocolate pot, exposing a hole in the lower lid that was just big enough for the skinny end of the molinet to slip through. A moment later, the lower lid was closed, the bumpy part of the molinet was hidden inside the pot, and she was rolling the slim, long wooden end of the tool vigorously between her hands. 'Never stint on this step,' she told me. 'Otherwise you'll lose all the froth.'

Oh, I wouldn't be stinting on any steps, not ever! I could tell that even before I'd taken a single sip.

'And now ...' She opened the lower lid, pulled out the molinet and closed the whole pot. 'If you'll pass me a cup ...'

I didn't even take a second to choose between all the different colourful patterns. I just grabbed the closest porcelain cup and handed it over.

Dark, frothy liquid filled it to the brim. It took all my willpower not to lunge as Marina finished pouring.

'One sip,' she told me. 'Only one, and I don't want you to swallow it all at once. Roll it around and take your time with it. Then tell me what you taste.'

My hands trembled with anticipation as I lifted the cup to my lips and closed my eyes. Slowly, reverently, I took my first taste and held it in my mouth, swirling it back and forth to savour every last drop. There was another, more subtle taste behind the deep, dark chocolate, something faint and warm that wasn't cinnamon, and it was growing ... growing ...

Ohhh! I almost dropped the cup as the hidden flavour exploded in my mouth like a fireball. It burned through my senses in a roar of flame until I swallowed it down without even meaning to and my eyes flew wide open. I was panting hard as I stared at Marina, my chest rising rapidly up and down. Flames licked through my body, almost like ... like ...

'*There*,' said Marina, in a tone of deep satisfaction. 'You haven't had that at any other chocolate houses, have you?'

'What was it?' I whispered. I couldn't find my voice.

She smiled smugly. 'That,' she said, 'is chilli chocolate. Our house speciality. What do you think?'

I didn't answer. But a sudden, startling wetness pricked at the back of my eyes.

I'd thought I would never feel that heat in my throat again. I'd thought that I had lost my flame forever.

Marina waited a moment and then nodded, as if satisfied by my response. 'All right,' she said. 'Drink the rest of it up, but don't take too long. That lazy lout Erik hadn't even finished grinding all the cocoa nibs for the day! It's a good thing you've eaten now, because there's plenty of work to be done, and believe me: you'll need all your strength to do it.'

The smile that stretched across my face when I heard that was completely uncontrollable.

I *could hardly wait.*

CHAPTER 10

By the time I'd been Marina's apprentice for a week, my puny human arms were stronger than I'd imagined possible. Every night, as I curled up by the fireplace to sleep on the warm kitchen floor, my muscles ached with effort, making me shift restlessly back and forth against my blankets and my scale-cloth to ease the burn.

But every single night, as smoke from the endlessly roasting cocoa beans circled around me, I closed my eyes and imagined that it was my family's smoky breath drifting over me, keeping me warm and safe in my new chocolate-filled home. Sometimes my eyes leaked again, as I thought of how it used to feel to fall asleep with Mother and Jasper's scaly bodies curled up next to mine. But sometimes just imagining their steady, hot breath against my skin was enough.

Chocolate followed me into my dreams, even when my family was there, too. Sometimes I was diving for jewels in our hoard with Jasper, racing to see who could find the most first, but mixed in with the gold and precious gems, I always found mountains and mountains of rough brown cocoa nibs, thirty times the size of the piles that I crushed and rolled into a liquid paste in the kitchen of the Chocolate Heart every day.

Sometimes I fell asleep to find myself curled up against the heat of my mother's great blue-and-gold back, her strong scales rising and falling under my snout as she spoke to me. Instead of Mother's voice, though, I heard Marina's, repeating the instructions that I'd memorised days ago: *You roll the nibs until they form a paste, and then you just keep on rolling with all your might, until not a single fraction of a bump, not a fragment of a shard of roughness, can even be remembered by it. In this chocolate house, you never stop until you've achieved perfection.*

And I never did stop until she told me it was time, not even when I had been rolling the paste for hours on the hot stone over the oven, the muscles in my hands seizing up and cramping as I pushed the heavy iron roller back and forth, back and forth, putting everything I had into the movements until the long muscles of my back would have screamed if they had had a voice.

Let them scream. All I cared about was the hot paste before me, growing smoother and smoother with every relentless pass of my roller.

Every time that Marina finally said, 'All right, stop,' her

words resonated inside me, filling me with as sweet a victory as if I'd finally launched into the air for my first flight.

I wasn't allowed to do the next stage of the work, not yet. Marina herself set the paste into round moulds, forming cakes of cooking chocolate that would have to wait a full month before they were used in the chocolate house. But every day when I passed the cupboard where the cakes were set, I sent silent, fierce whispers to the ones that had been made from my paste. *Be strong. Be right.*

I was counting down the days until the first of them could be used. I only hoped that Marina would let me taste what was made from that one, to see for myself how I'd done.

But I had more than enough work to keep me busy in the meantime.

There were always cocoa beans roasting over the open fire, and it was my job to deal with them. They started out as plain, unimpressive beans that would never have caught my eye for an instant as a dragon, but they were carried into the chocolate house in sacks that we treated just as reverently as if they had been filled with gold. It was like magic, how those plain, ordinary-looking beans could hold the rich secret of chocolate inside them.

I was the one who took them out of the hot roaster when they were finally ready to reveal that secret, like dragon eggs getting ready to hatch. Marina stood over me, watching every move, the first three times I pierced their thin, crackly outer shells to pull out the cocoa nibs we needed. A single slip of my hands, and the precious nib would be ruined, the chocolate essence lost as if it had never existed. Even the thought of it was enough to fill me with panic. It would be like smashing a diamond tiara through sheer carelessness. I was only too glad to have Marina there to save me from making any mistakes.

But the fourth time I prepared the roasted beans for shelling, Marina only raised her face-fur – no, *eyebrows* – at me from across the kitchen, where she was preparing an assortment of chocolate creams for our morning customers. 'Well?' she said. 'What are you waiting for? Get on with it.'

So – after a startled moment – I did.

And that felt an awful lot like flying, too.

On the seventh day of my apprenticeship, Horst walked into the kitchen and clapped one hand to his head with a groan of horror. '*Marina!*'

'What now?' Marina didn't even bother to look up from the kettle where she was combining ingredients for her special chilli chocolate. 'Have the customers complained? Has the king himself decided to visit? Or are you just here to make my life difficult again?'

'Not you,' Horst said, through gritted teeth. 'Her!' He pointed at me.

I blinked, but I didn't stop grinding the big white sugar loaf I was working on. It needed to be crushed into fine powder to dissolve into Marina's concoctions, and it was still a nearly eight-inch-long solid lump.

'What about her?' Marina said. 'Unlike the last one, she's not a disaster. So far.'

'So far?' He let out a hiss of exasperation. 'Have you even noticed that this is her seventh day of work in a row? And I haven't noticed her leave for any afternoons off.'

Afternoons off? What was he talking about? I frowned at him even as my hands and arms continued in their grinding.

Horst looked from one to the other of us and groaned again, shaking his head. 'Every apprentice,' he said, holding up one forefinger, 'receives one afternoon off a week, by law, along with two full days a month. Remember?'

Marina tapped a sliver of dark red powder into the kettle. 'I'm not stopping her. If she wants to find something more interesting to do ...'

More interesting than chocolate? I *don't think so.* I turned over the sugar loaf, starting a new angle of attack.

'Look –' Horst began, through his teeth. Then he stopped. 'What's your apprentice's name, Marina?'

Marina shrugged. 'I don't know. It hasn't come up.'

'It *hasn't* – ?!'

'What's your name, girl?' Marina called out.

For a moment my hands stilled in their work as I remembered Silke's words: '*How about we call you Eva? That's a nice ordinary name, with no mysteries.*'

If there was one thing Silke understood, it was people, and how to manage them. 'I'm –'

Then I slammed my lips shut, my skin suddenly hot and pricklingly aware of my scale-cloth, lying folded in the storage cupboard across the room. Hidden ... but not abandoned. Never abandoned.

Some things were more important than fitting in.

'I'm Aventurine,' I told them firmly.

'Aven– sorry, what?' Horst frowned.

'*Aventurine*,' Marina said firmly. 'You heard her. Now, do you have something to say to us, or are you just bored with mollycoddling rich people and want to see some real work for once?'

Horst sighed heavily. 'I am here,' he said, 'to make certain that the lord mayor's men can't find any violations to report to the merchants' guild, which is exactly what they're itching to do. Apparently, *someone* managed to make our esteemed local leader furious by firing his nephew.' He gave Marina a meaningful look. 'Two of his assistants have been sniffing around outside since eight o'clock this morning, looking for something to complain about. I wouldn't be surprised if they send someone in here for an out-of-the-blue kitchen inspection, too.'

'Just let them try,' Marina said darkly. She'd stopped adding ingredients to her mix, though. Her lips pursed for a moment, and then she nodded decisively. 'Fine. Aventurine?' She jerked her head in the direction of the door. 'Out!'

'What?' I stared at her, still grinding the sugar loaf. 'But I'm not done. I still need to –'

'Go and have some fun that isn't chocolate flavoured,' Marina told me. 'Lord mayor's orders.' She snorted. 'Enjoy. Don't come back after dark, though, or you'll find the shop locked and you'll have to throw pebbles at my window to get my attention. And I'm not staying in all night to wait for you, I'll tell you that right now.'

I gave her a flat stare. 'I don't want to leave in the first place. This is ridiculous! I don't even *want* an afternoon off.'

'Well, I don't want to be hauled up in front of the town council for an ear-hammering, just because my apprentice happens to be as stubborn as a donkey!' said Marina.

'She's not the only one,' Horst muttered.

Marina pointed one finger at the door and gave me a narrow look. 'Well?'

Growling, I pulled off my apron. 'Can't I just finish the sugar and – ?'

'Don't worry about any of that.' Horst's shoulders relaxed and he tossed me a coin. 'Here, your first week's wages. Now go and enjoy yourself. Marina can take care of everything here that needs doing. Believe me, she's had more than enough practice at managing it all herself, every time she terrifies away another one of her apprentices.'

'I am not terrified,' I snarled. 'Just very, very irritated at the waste of my time when I could be getting some work done!' Slapping down my apron, I stalked towards the doors.

'Oh, wonderful,' Horst mumbled. 'Now we have two of them.'

I slammed the kitchen doors shut behind me.

There were four customers sitting in the front room, along with a small, thin man who was walking restlessly around, frowning as he ran his fingers over the painted walls, and a brown-haired woman loitering outside, peering in through the windows. I would have assumed she was just dithering about whether or not to come in, but as I

94

stepped through the front door she coughed meaningfully and crooked one beringed finger at me.

It took me a moment of bafflement – and then outrage – to realise that she was actually trying to summon me with that gesture.

It was lucky for her, considering my mood, that I didn't have the power of flame any more. As it was, I gave her a look that should have singed her eyebrows off.

'I'm a chocolatier, not a waitress,' I informed her. 'And anyway, it's my *afternoon off*.' Seething, I turned on one heel and started in the opposite direction.

'Wait!' Long fingers closed around my arm and dragged me back, past the front window, until no one inside the chocolate house could see us. Sharp nails bit through the cloth of my dress when I tried to yank myself away. 'There's no need to take offence, my little chocolatier. I only want to get to know you.' The woman's pale pink lips curved in a smile, but her green eyes flicked up and down my face with the cold intelligence of a predator sizing up its next meal. 'You're the new apprentice, aren't you? That must be a difficult job, especially for a young girl on her own.'

My eyes narrowed and I stopped trying to pull free. 'Are you trying to steal it for yourself?' I demanded.

'Me? At my age?' She let out a choke of startled-sounding laughter. 'I don't think so. I'm a bit older than twelve, you know. And besides, I hear this chocolatier mistreats her apprentices. I hear a lot of other things, too … and you might find I'm a sympathetic listener.'

She cocked her head, her pink smile stretching wider.

'Apprentices don't make much money, and this is an expensive city. Perhaps life could become a little easier for you if I offered to pay you for your time? And, of course, for any little titbits you care to let drop that I might find particularly interesting ... any nasty, embarrassing little secrets that your tyrant of an employer might be trying to hide ... ?' She raised her eyebrows. 'The lord mayor himself would owe you his deepest appreciation.'

Oh. Now I did understand.

Jasper's human philosophers might not have cared about chocolate, but they'd talked on and on about scheming and corruption.

Just to make absolutely certain, though, I looked her straight in the eyes and said, 'So you'll pay me to tell you something bad about Marina? Something the lord mayor can use to get her into trouble?'

'I'd need to give you some compensation for your help, wouldn't I?' Her voice poured through the air, as sweet as cream mixed with sugar. 'And if you were willing to swear to that information in front of the town council, well ... who knows what opportunities might be available for a child who proved so helpful and loyal to her city?'

'I understand.' I nodded.

'Oh, good! I was certain you'd be clever enough to help me.' Her fingers dropped away as she stepped back, gesturing down the street. 'Let's just go this way and find a cosy little cafe where you can tell me everything, eh?'

'Actually,' I said, 'I'd rather tell you now.' I smiled at her with all my teeth bared, which should have warned her.

Then I lashed out with one foot and kicked her hard.

'Aaargh!' Shrieking, she dropped down to clutch her leg.

It was pathetic. I didn't even have claws on my human feet, so she was barely damaged. My mother would have been ashamed of me for such a weak attack.

Still, I had my head start. I turned and ran.

I could hear her cursing as she started after me a moment later, but I was too fast for her to catch. As I passed the front window of the Chocolate Heart, I saw Horst hurrying towards the door, wide-eyed and open-mouthed with what looked like horror. But I didn't run back to him and to safety ... and not just because I'd been ordered to spend the next few hours out.

Scales or not, I was still a dragon. There was no chance in the world that I was going to sit back and let anyone threaten my hoard.

So it was a good thing that I had an afternoon off after all. I knew exactly how to use it.

CHAPTER 11

The grey sky was full of clouds, and mud sucked wetly at my feet as I walked along the riverbank, but the market where Silke's brother worked was still heaving with customers. I had to wait until he had finished serving a large, bickering family before I could finally leave my message with him.

'Let Silke know I'm looking for her,' I said. 'And tell her we can help each other this time.'

'Oh, good,' he said wearily. His dark brown face was shadowed by the cloth that hung over his stall to protect the clothing on his table, and he didn't bother to look up at me as he sorted out the money from his last customers, peering down at their coins through a pair of spectacles that looked ready to fall off his nose at any moment. 'May I also tell her *who* is looking for her?' he asked. 'Or how to find you – if she even wants to?'

'Just tell her,' I told him, 'that I gave her my very last coin, but it was worth it after all. Oh, and I decided to keep my name.'

I knew my prey. Easy answers weren't what she was looking for. She'd solve the puzzle in a heartbeat – and she would want the story of what had happened next, after I'd disappeared into the Chocolate Heart a week ago. Silke's curiosity was like dragonfire inside her.

But her brother looked far less satisfied than I felt.

'Oh, of course. Because *that* isn't at all mysterious!' He picked up a rumpled garment that one of his shoppers had discarded, and he shook it out with a snap that cracked through the air. 'My little sister and her secrets! If she ever stayed in one place like a normal person ...'

'Will you tell her?' I asked.

He sighed heavily. 'Of course I will. But I can't make any promises about when I'll see her next. She drops in and out all day, as she likes.'

'That's fine.' I had been working since dawn. 'I'm getting hungry anyway.'

Silke found me half an hour later and four streets away, as I stood outside a colourful flower shop, munching on a hot salted pretzel from an open street-oven while melted butter trickled down my fingers.

I heard her voice before I saw her. 'You'll need a second dress soon, you know. You can't wear the same thing every day without people noticing.'

I shrugged my shoulders without turning around. 'My employer doesn't seem to mind.' Marina would care if I started to stink, of course – cleanliness around the kitchen was one of her most important rules – but I changed into my scale-cloth every few nights so that I could wash my dress, and it all seemed to be working out so far. In fact, Marina probably wouldn't notice if I wore the scale-cloth all day long, as long as I kept on following her orders. On the other hand ...

'I'll think about buying another dress,' I told Silke. 'And I'll even do it from your family's stall to help you out ... *if* you can help out my business, too.'

'Your business, eh?' Silke was smiling as she finally moved into view, wearing a long black jacket that swished around her as she walked. 'All right, you've caught my interest.' She reached out and tore off one corner of my pretzel with quick, long brown fingers. 'So, tell me, *Aventurine*, how in the world you managed to get yourself invited into the back room of that chocolate house last week, and exactly what position they've given you. Scullery maid? Errand girl?'

'Neither,' I said smugly, and pulled the rest of the pretzel safely out of Silke's reach. 'I'm Marina's new apprentice.'

'*What?*' Silke's fingers went still in mid-air, with her stolen pretzel piece hovering just outside her mouth. '*You're* an apprentice chocolatier?' She stared at me. 'Do you have any idea how hard it is to get an ordinary apprenticeship in this city – even for girls with family connections and fine manners? To be taken on as an apprentice chocolatier of all things – ! Even if your mistress *is* a nightmare – !' She shook her head in visible amazement. 'How did you manage it?'

'Because I'm not ordinary,' I snapped. 'And Marina is *not* a nightmare!' If I'd been in my proper shape, tendrils of smoke would have flown out of my nostrils in warning at that insult.

But Silke didn't even seem to realise she was in danger. 'Oh, I'm just repeating what everyone in the city says,' she told me cheerfully, as she finally started nibbling on her stolen morsel. 'I asked around about her last week, you know, after you disappeared in there. I got curious.'

What a surprise. I chomped ferociously down on the rest of my pretzel, wishing I had sharper teeth. *Then* I'd look really menacing!

Silke didn't look in the slightest bit intimidated, though, as she licked melted butter off her fingers. 'Apparently,' she told me, in between licks, 'when the richest banker in town came to the Chocolate Heart with his wife, your mistress actually *refused* to come out and speak to them afterwards, when they wanted to compliment her chocolate. Can you believe it? The banker's wife said she'd never been so offended in her life. She told everyone she knew never to go back there!'

'Then she was a fool.' I snorted as I wiped my hands off on my dress. 'Marina can't leave the kitchen to have a chat when she's in the middle of making chocolate. It's a delicate procedure.'

'Oh, and that's another thing!' Silke shook her head

disapprovingly. 'She won't allow anyone else into her kitchen, will she? People absolutely *hate* that.'

'You think she should let outsiders into her *kitchen?*' I stared at her in disbelief. 'Who would be stupid enough to do that?'

'*Everyone* does that.' Silke rolled her eyes. 'Everyone with any business sense, I mean. It makes the customers happy, but apparently your mistress doesn't care about that. Because – and this is the worst of all – when the lord mayor himself asked her to make a special chocolate drink for his inauguration, *she refused him*. She said the ingredients he'd suggested would be inedible! Can you imagine?'

'Yes!' I snarled. 'Yes, I can.' My eyes had turned to narrow slits and I was longing for the power of flame. 'I'm sure they would have been disgusting. For anyone who doesn't know about chocolate to try to design a new drink –'

'Yes, yes, of course it would have been terrible.' Sticking her hands in her pockets, Silke rocked back on the heels of her boots. 'But she didn't have to *tell* him that, did she? She could have made something of her own and just given him the credit, like any sensible businesswoman would have. Instead she insulted him – *him*, the most important man in the city, apart from the king! – and now none of the other merchants will ever hire her either. I heard that the lord mayor said afterwards, if it wasn't for the fact that his own nephew was her apprentice, he'd – *oh*. Wait. Wait!' Her eyebrows shot upward. 'Of course. So *that's* why you need my help!'

I hated being in a position of weakness. I crossed my

arms and squared my shoulders, making myself as big as possible. 'The lord mayor is trying to shut us down,' I told her flatly. 'We need to get people on our side.'

I might have been busy in the kitchen, but I hadn't failed to notice how few customers sat scattered around the warm, fire-coloured front room of the Chocolate Heart, compared to the aristocratic crowds who'd filled those snooty chocolate houses in the first district. Chocolate houses ran on money, just like the rest of human society, and customers – no matter how annoying they might be – brought in silver coins and support.

With the lord mayor scheming against us now, we needed all the support we could get.

'Ohhhh.' Silke leaned back against the wall of the flower shop, between buckets full of blue and pink and purple blooms, and braced herself on her outstretched legs. Her eyes turned dreamy and unfocused. 'Oh yes, I see. In that case ...'

'Yes?' I leaned forward.

'You'll need a whole flood of new customers as quickly as possible,' she said. 'Influential ones, too. And better yet, they should all start talking as loudly as they can about how wonderful you are, until you're far too famous for him to quietly shut down.'

'And?' I stared at her, desperately trying to read her expression. This was what I'd come for. This was *why* I'd come to the one human I knew who was the best at manipulation. 'Can you do it?'

Silke's sharp gaze snapped on to mine. Her lips curved into an even sharper grin. 'Oh, this is going to be a *challenge*,' she told me. 'And I'll warn you right now: I'm going to need a lot more than one little dress purchase from you as payment.'

Silke really did know this entire city. As she asked me thousands of questions about the Chocolate Heart for 'research', figuring out how to make other people love it as much as I did, she led me from one colourful neighbourhood to another, moving with easy confidence through the crowds. Tradesman after tradeswoman greeted her by name on all the different streets, and I could see her taking in every detail around her, even as she bombarded me with surprisingly intelligent questions about the chocolate house ... and slipped in more than a few sidelong questions about my own past, too.

Of course, I didn't tell her anything about that. I might be starting to trust one or two select humans, but the secret of my true nature was mine alone. Still, I found myself enjoying the battle, as she tried different sneaky tactics to get me to reveal the truth about myself, and I sidestepped her questions every time. It felt like play-fighting with words instead of claws – and she was the first worthy opponent I'd had since I'd changed shape.

After her final attempt, she grinned and shook her head, and I surprised myself by grinning back at her.

'Never mind,' she said. 'You're determined to stay a mystery, but I'll figure you out one day, just like I've figured out your chocolate house. And in the meantime, you can leave your problem with me.' She glanced up at the mid-afternoon sky and sighed. 'I need to get back to the riverbank now, or Dieter will have a fit. But don't worry, Aventurine ... you'll be hearing from me very soon.'

I could almost hear her brain whirring with new schemes as she sauntered off, whistling to herself.

Still smiling, I turned around.

Dragons didn't need human friends, obviously. But if I did ...

Well, she would be a good one to have.

I had work of my own to do now, if I was going to talk Marina and Horst into providing the payment I'd promised Silke, but I couldn't start yet. I was under orders to stay out of the Chocolate Heart all afternoon, and if there was one thing Marina expected from her apprentice, it was obedience. So, instead of starting back towards home, I wandered slowly through the streets of Drachenburg, taking in all the strange sights of the human city.

I'd learned an awful lot of new words and concepts over the past week. But I still hadn't stopped being surprised by what humans did with them.

Almost everything I could imagine was on sale in the shops of Drachenburg, and even more things that I would never have imagined. As I wandered from one district to another, looking into every window I passed, I saw towering cakes and tiny glass bottles that reeked of so much artificial scent they made me sneeze just from the whiffs I caught through open shop doors. There were bright, light-coloured cafes full of chatting women and children, and dark-panelled restaurants full of men and smoke and newspapers, and there were shops crammed with so many full bookshelves my brother Jasper would have roared with greed.

I even spotted, strangest of all, one shop window full of toys where a row of tiny wooden men marched back and forth again and again, carrying minuscule weapons by their sides. Orange-and-green wooden dragons waved their painted wings threateningly at the tiny men from the corners of the window, with red drops like blood trickling down their painted chins.

I envied those dragons so much it hurt.

I would have stopped longer to watch the odd toys – Grandfather had never brought home anything like that! – but I was shoved aside only a moment later by a crowd of chattering human children with an older, grey-haired woman who sighed and shrugged her shoulders at me as they all pushed past and wrestled each other for space in front of the glass.

And it wasn't only the shops that were crowded. Even the lamp posts here were covered with paper handbills that had been plastered or nailed on to advertise different shops and events. More bits of paper fluttered across the cobbled street, falling under the horses' hoofs and being stepped on by the masses and masses of people who surged back and forth in endless waves of motion.

Dragons would never choose to live crammed together with thousands and thousands of other creatures, with no space to spread their wings or roar out a claim on a real, open territory of their own.

Didn't anyone here want room to breathe?

Even as I thought that, slowing to frown at the crowd around me, a noisy group of men shoved past me from behind, pushing so close that I had to leap aside at the last moment to save myself from being knocked over. I opened my mouth to snarl at them – but the sight of their telltale black robes made my mouth slam shut and my chest squeeze tight with sudden panic as I froze in place, like a helpless prey animal with nowhere to hide.

Battle mages! I'd spent all my life being warned against them. *'Don't ever let them spot you,'* Grandfather had told us. *'Until your scales are at least a hundred years hardened, turn and fly away as fast as you can whenever you see those black coverings!'*

But these battle mages had no idea that they were passing a secret dragon. They didn't even glance at me as they stalked past. They were far too busy with their debate.

'No matter what the king thinks, we can't pretend this isn't happening. That's five sightings over the outer provinces now! Something has set off those beasts for the first time in decades. If they're getting ready for a serious attack –'

'They haven't attacked any humans in decades!'

'But we have to be ready. If we attacked first and took them off guard –'

'Maybe we could soften their scales with a dissolving poison –'

'Or turn their fire inwards –'

Eurgggh! Horror clenched my stomach, nearly doubling me over, as their voices faded out of earshot, their robes disappearing into the crowd.

That was my family they'd been talking about!

Whatever they try, it won't work, I told myself. *It won't, it won't, it can't!* The words ran over themselves in a panicked babble in my mind as I tried desperately to believe them. *They can't get through full-grown dragon scales. Stupid mages. My family would eat them if they ever tried!*

And I wouldn't give them the benefit of my fear. No!

I forced myself to straighten up – and nearly bumped into a group of women in billowing dresses on my left. I pulled back just in time, but they didn't seem to notice our near collision. None of them even blinked as they swept past me, continuing their own conversations as if nothing had happened. I had to keep moving, too, or I would be bowled over by the crowd surging behind me.

Thank goodness I would be able to retreat to our kitchen as soon as this maddening 'afternoon off' was finally over. But right here and now, stuck in these too-close crowds with no chocolate to save me ...

I tilted my head back to look longingly past the city's clustered rooftops to the great green foothills in the grey drizzly distance, past the massive clock tower. The clouds were so low and heavy today, I could only spot the beginning of my family's mountain range as a speck of darkness far away, hidden behind the grey mist. If I hadn't known what I was looking at, I would have thought ...

I blinked. Then I rubbed my eyes, my breath stopping in my throat.

Had that speck just moved? *Yes!* It was coming closer! It –

No.

The clouds shifted, and I let out my breath in a rush that felt like a punch to my chest.

The mountain range rose, steady and impenetrable in the distance. It had only been a trick of the light that made me think I saw anything else.

Stupid. Stupid, stupid, stupid! I dug my nails into my palm like claws.

My family might have been spotted flying out in the provinces, but they would never show themselves so close to a real human city. And this was the *capital* city at that, the home of the king and his whole court and army. Grandfather would never allow such foolishness ... and of course I would never expect him to.

So there was no reason in the world for my puny human chest to suddenly ache or for water to well up in my weak human eyes.

Was I actually *crying*, here, in public? I clenched my jaw tight and forced back the tears.

It hurt more than swallowing fire. But I was a dragon. I was mighty.

I blinked hard and forced myself forward through the crush of humans, letting their chatter and their smells and their overwhelming closeness wash over me.

I was still the fiercest creature in this city.

But I didn't let myself look towards the mountain again.

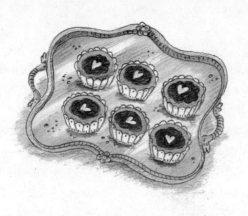

CHAPTER 12

By the time I finally returned to the Chocolate Heart, the grey skies were shifting into a dark, murky charcoal, the air had turned thick and cold, and the chocolate house was closed for the day. I had to hammer on the locked door for Marina to come and let me in through the darkened front room.

Luckily, she hadn't yet gone upstairs to her apartment for the night. The candles were still lit in the warm kitchen, where Horst sat drinking chocolate at a table that had been pulled in from the front room, along with two chairs and a sheet of paper with what looked like a recipe scrawled in fresh ink. As I followed Marina inside, he looked up at me with his half-full porcelain cup cradled in both hands.

'Please,' he said to me, 'for the sake of my heart, tell me that wasn't you I saw having an actual, physical altercation with one of the lord mayor's assistants outside our shop earlier?'

'"Altercation?"' I blinked at him, trying to figure out the unfamiliar word. My brain felt as chilled-through as my body and filled with grey fog.

'A fight,' Marina said drily, sitting back down across from him. She lifted her own cup from the table as she asked me, 'Did you get in any good punches at least?'

'No,' I said regretfully. 'I only kicked her.'

'Oh God!' Horst's head landed beside the sheet of paper with a thud. 'Marina ...' he moaned.

'Shh.' She looked at me, her eyes narrowing. I don't know what she saw in my face, but she pushed her cup of chocolate towards me. 'Here,' she said. 'You look as if you need it.'

'*She* needs it?' Horst mumbled against the table. 'When the lord mayor's constables arrive tomorrow to arrest our apprentice for her unprovoked attack, and claim that we ordered her to do it ...'

'They're not going to arrest her,' Marina said briskly. 'I'll bet you anything I'd find a bruise on at least one of Aventurine's arms, underneath those ugly sleeves. People kick when they're trying to get away, not to attack. Isn't that right, apprentice?'

I scowled as I sat down on the floor to drink, my purple-and-gold skirts billowing around me. 'My sleeves aren't ugly,' I muttered.

'You just keep on telling yourself that,' said Marina. She stood up and started pulling out pots and pans from the cupboards, letting them clatter against each other. 'So, where exactly was our beloved lord mayor's assistant trying to take you, before you kicked your way to freedom?'

I shrugged and took a long sip of Marina's hot chocolate. It had extra chilli in it today, and I swallowed down the flames with gratitude, letting them warm me from the inside out. 'Some cafe, I think,' I told Marina.

'Oh, well, *that* was certainly worth kicking a public servant over,' Horst muttered. 'Thank goodness you escaped that horror. Who knows what might have happened there? She might even have forced you to eat cake!'

'It would have been dry and tasteless,' Marina told him. 'The closest cafe is Florian's, remember? They never put enough syrup in their batter.'

'Oh, for – !'

I spoke over Horst's bellow. 'She wanted me to betray you.'

As Horst broke off and turned to stare at me, I gripped my hot cup in both hands and breathed in its steam. I needed it to wash away the grim grey chill that had filled me ever since that terrible sight of wings-that-weren't.

I soaked in the bright warmth of Marina's white kitchen, the scent of the roasting cocoa beans, and Marina bustling by one of the stoves, measuring out cream with a generous hand, as if the whole vista could wash away the grey from my heart in a brilliant swathe of colour.

This was where I belonged now. This was who I was. And I wouldn't let anyone take it from me. 'She offered me money,' I told Marina and Horst, 'and told me that I'd have the lord mayor's gratitude if I made up any nasty secrets about your kitchen and then testified about them in front of the town council.'

The clattering at the stove abruptly stopped. Marina's hand had stilled in mid-air. 'Well, now,' she said, 'that *is* a surprise. I would have expected that little termite Erik to make up all the stories they could want, without anyone needing to turn to you.'

'Stories from Erik wouldn't count,' Horst told her. 'Not after the whole street watched you toss him out on his ear.' He looked down at his hot chocolate with a wry smile on his face. 'Perhaps it's just as well you weren't polite or quiet about getting rid of him, after all. At least this way every shop owner in the district knows he bears a grudge against you. The council would never trust any testimony from him against you now.'

'Ha,' said Marina. She pulled over the bowl of crushed sugar. 'I'm going to remind you of that next time you natter on at me about my manners.'

Horst sighed. 'Then I'm sure you'll have plenty of opportunities. Still, as long as you remember to stay away from the customers ...'

'And why would I ever want to go near them?' Rolling her eyes, Marina picked up a long wooden spoon. 'Come along,' she told me. 'Finish up that cup, and quickly now. I'm going to teach you a new recipe.'

'My recipe?' Horst said hopefully. He lifted the piece of paper from the table in front of him. 'Because I really think –'

'I'll let you play in my kitchen,' said Marina, 'the day you send me out front to take care of the public.'

'Ouch!' Horst gave a dramatic shudder. 'Now you're simply being cruel.'

'Hmmph.' Marina shook her head at him. But as she turned away I saw a grin twitching at the corners of her mouth.

Horst was grinning, too, looking more relaxed than I'd ever seen him ... but when I obediently stood up from the table, holding my half-drunk cup of hot chocolate, his face suddenly tightened into a frown. 'Wait. Marina, do you even realise what time it is? Most apprentices –'

'Of course I know the time,' said Marina. 'It's evening. That means her afternoon off is finished, doesn't it? So she can stop lazing around and get back to work.'

'Oh yes,' I said with sincere gratitude. I drank the last of my hot chocolate in one fiery gulp. 'It is *definitely* time to work.'

Nothing could distract me from my feelings better than the scent of chocolate. Over the next few days I buried myself in it until I could barely even recognise anything else.

So I was startled, four days later, when Horst stepped through the swinging doors and looked at me with a frown on his face. 'Someone,' he said, 'is here to see you.'

'Me?' I was stirring a pot of chocolate cream, and I couldn't stop even for a moment, but I frowned back at him and shook my head. 'There must be a mistake.'

'Thanks *very* much,' said Silke, stepping in behind him. 'Have you forgotten all our plans already?' Today she was wearing a flamboyant red jacket over plain black trousers, and her hands rested casually in her pockets, but her eyes looked wider than usual, and her face younger, as she gazed around the kitchen. 'I have to say, Aventurine, I'm impressed.'

'Ungggh.' Horst sounded pained. 'Marina ...'

'Here.' Marina handed him a tray of hot chocolates. 'Go and suck up to rich people and be happy. Shoo!' Then she turned to scowl at me as the doors swung shut behind Horst, leaving her alone with me and Silke in the kitchen. 'Tell me, apprentice,' she said, her tone deceptively gentle, 'did I hire you to hold tea parties in my kitchen?'

'Oh, this isn't a social visit.' Silke pulled her hands out of her pockets and gave Marina a jaunty bow. 'It's more in the way of a business update. I take it Aventurine's told you all about my commission?'

Marina didn't answer. But she turned towards me with her eyebrows raised, and I could feel a dangerous storm cloud brewing in the air.

Oh, stones and bones. 'I forgot,' I said, and gritted my teeth as Silke raised her own eyebrows at me, too, joining in the sisterhood of disapproval. 'I've been busy!'

'Busier than usual.' Marina's eyes narrowed. She swung around to face Silke. 'Do you have anything to do with that, girl?'

'We-e-elll ...' Silke grinned as she whipped out a piece of paper from an inside pocket of her jacket. 'I thought I'd stop by and let you all have an eyeful of this. You'd be surprised just how many copies people have been passing all around the city, ever since they first appeared yesterday morning.'

'Oh?' Marina took Silke's paper before I could even reach for it. 'Hmm.' Frowning, she glanced up and down ... then, frowning harder, turned her gaze back to the top and read it through again.

I waited, still stirring the pot of chocolate cream and feeling a first, small itch of curiosity ripple through me, breaking through the self-imposed numbness of my last few days. The satisfied smile on Silke's face told its own story as she stood with her hands clasped behind her back, bouncing gently on her toes.

There had been a lot more orders coming into the kitchen than usual, come to think of it.

I *hadn't* thought about it, personally, because I'd been shutting my mind to absolutely everything but chocolate. It was the only safe thing I could let myself think about, after waking every morning from frantic dreams of searching through endless tunnels in my home mountain while my family called out to me, too far away to reach.

I hated those dreams. It was almost as if they *wanted* to make me miserable, which was utterly ridiculous and completely unfair. There was a good reason I didn't let myself think about those things when I was awake. It was bad enough that I'd lost my family, without having to have all these *feelings* about it!

It was enough to make me give up on my brain forever.

But Horst had just carried out nine hot chocolates at once to the front room, and we'd made another load to order just beforehand. There were customers waiting now for eight glasses of sweet chocolate cream.

So in the last twenty-four hours, while I hadn't been paying attention to the world around me, something had definitely changed.

'What does it say?' I demanded, when I finally lost my patience.

'You'd better see for yourself.' Marina pursed her lips as she passed it over. 'Especially if you're responsible for it.'

'Ahem.' Silke cleared her throat. 'Actually, Aventurine is only *partially* responsible for it. You see, she commissioned me to take care of your problem, but when it came to the actual solution, along with the writing and production ...'

I let her voice fade into the background as I looked down at the paper in my hands. It was a printed handbill, the kind that seemed to float all over the city, lying discarded on pavements and plastered on lamp posts, and it read, in elegant, curling type:

Let it hereby be recorded that, despite every rumour to the contrary, the chocolatier at the Chocolate Heart has never admitted to being a food mage herself. Nor has she ever publicly or privately agreed with those who claim that a food mage must have been involved in the creation of her exceptional chocolate. She wishes the public to know that she is both shocked and outraged by the

*incredible claims that have been made about her famously
fiery hot chocolates and other rich and extraordinary
delicacies offered exclusively at: The Chocolate Heart,
No. 13 Koenigstrasse, in the Third District.*

*Of course, as her kitchen is kept notoriously private,
with no visitors ever allowed inside, no absolute evidence
can be provided of her chocolate's non-magical origins.
However, we are certain that all right-minded citizens
will be more than happy to accept the famously reclusive
and mysterious chocolatier's assertions that no magic was
involved in the creation of such mouth-watering bliss, no
matter how unlikely that claim may seem ...*

I turned the page, but the writing didn't continue. It just
left off with those dangling ellipses, implying ... something.
I didn't like it. Just the thought of food mages made it hard
for me to breathe. My back itched like fire where my wings
ought to have been rooted in my skin. I had to shift my
shoulders irritably to make sure that they were still gone.
'What is this?'

'It's piffle,' Marina snarled. 'That's what it is.'

'It's *marketing*,' Silke said, 'and it's brilliant.' She beamed
at us. 'So, about my payment ... ?'

'Marketing?' Marina threw up her hands. 'Smears and
libels, more like! As if I couldn't come up with my own
chocolate without the help of some lazy food mage lounging
around my kitchen –'

'But it says you *didn't* use a food mage,' I told her,
pointing at the page. 'Look: it says that lots of times.'

'You think so?' She seized the paper from me, growling. 'Well, look again, missy, and this time, use your head. These words may *say* one thing, but they *mean* the opposite.'

'It's perfect!' Silke said. 'No one, not even the lord mayor himself, could argue that you've made any false claims.'

'But everyone who reads this piece of nonsense is going to think I'm hiding a food mage in my kitchen!' Marina whirled around, waving the paper accusingly. 'I don't know how you came up with this idea at your age, girl, much less how you managed to get it printed, but of all the outrageous, uncalled-for, misguided and ridiculous – !'

The swinging doors opened, and Horst stepped into the kitchen, looking so pale and shaken that even Marina cut off her tirade as the doors fell closed behind him.

'Well?' she snapped. 'What now? What new disaster?'

Horst didn't speak. He lifted his hand. It shivered in mid-air, holding a familiar white handbill.

'Oh, so that's all,' said Marina. 'I know, it's absurd, but –'

'No,' Horst croaked, his voice rusty, 'that isn't it.' The handbill fluttered from his hand to the ground, and he blinked down at it as if he didn't even know how it had got there. 'I mean ...' He ran one trembling hand over his short, tight, black curls and took a deep breath. When he spoke again, his voice had settled back into its normal deep tones. 'That handbill's a brilliant piece of work, obviously, and we need to find whoever wrote it and thank them forever –'

'A-*ha*!' Silke smiled smugly. 'As I was saying – !'

'But ...' Horst didn't even seem to hear her interruption as he looked back up at Marina, swallowing convulsively.

'Right now, out there, we have new customers, brought in by that handbill,' he told her, 'and an urgent order for three of your finest hot chocolates. *Immediately*.'

'Oh, they're always in a hurry, aren't they? *Customers.*' Scowling, Marina shrugged her big shoulders and turned back to the stove. 'Well, they can join the queue and they'll get their drinks when I'm ready. I still need to finish off these chocolate creams, and then –'

'These particular hot chocolates can't wait,' said Horst. For the first time since I'd known him, his lips twitched and stretched into a smile of pure wonder, until he looked ten years younger and ready to float off his feet with excitement. 'You see, they've been ordered by the two princesses and the king himself.'

CHAPTER 13

'What?' Silke let out a squeak of excitement so unguarded I could hardly believe it came from her. 'The royal family read *my handbill*? Oh, I knew it was good, but I never really –'

'Are they wearing their crowns?' I asked, perking up. Now *that* would be something worth seeing ... and maybe more. My fingers tingled with the memory of all the lovely gold crowns in my family's hoard. They'd looped so neatly around my claws, clicking together with my every movement. Even the plain ones were delightful, but the ones encrusted with precious gems were my favourites.

It would be so much easier to go to sleep at night with a crown or two tucked against my side, just like in the old days!

But no. I gritted my teeth together and forced myself to think like a human, not a dragon. Trapped inside this puny body, without sharp teeth, claws or flame on my side, there was no possible way for me to seize the crowns from the royal family's heads and keep them. Still, it was so hard to push down the roar of greed that wanted to billow up through my throat as I thought of all that lovely gold just waiting to be made my own and ...

'Don't you dare stop stirring, girl!' snapped Marina.

I jolted back into action just in time to stop the pot of chocolate cream from boiling ... and to hear Horst say, 'They're incognito.'

'They're *what*?' Was he saying that my wonderful crowns were ruined?

He waved one dark hand impatiently. '*Incognito* means *in disguise*.' He turned to Marina. 'A messenger boy came by this morning to make a reservation for "Count von Reimann" and his daughters. They're dressed like any other nobles, but the moment I saw them step inside, I knew exactly who they were, and so did everyone else. I wouldn't be surprised if there are scribblers from the newspapers hurrying over here right now. We already have a crowd piling up outside just to peer through our front windows!'

'Sounds like a pretty manky disguise then.' Snorting, Marina elbowed me aside to take over the last stages of the chocolate creams. 'Maybe next time they should think about wearing masks.'

'Oh, being incognito is only for show.' Silke spoke with a knowledgeable air, rocking back and forth on her heels with her hands tucked in her pockets. 'If they came as themselves, they'd have to bring along a whole honour guard. This way, they can travel without so many soldiers and servants cluttering things up. But ...'

Her eyes widened, and she lost her poise. 'Ahh!' She clapped her hands to her cheeks. 'I can't believe the king himself read my handbill! The *king himself*! Is there any way to see into the front room from here? I want to see the crown princess! I've never been this close to her before!'

For the first time since I'd met him, Horst looked mischievous. 'If you want a *really* good view ...' Reaching over to the wall, he lifted a decorative plate from a hook just higher than my head. Behind it was an inch-wide square of clear glass. 'Just this once,' he told us both, winking, 'but be quick. No one wants to see eyeballs peering in at them as they eat!'

'Come on!' Silke grabbed my arm and pulled me with her. 'Ohhhhh.' She pressed her eye against the glass and hummed with satisfaction. 'She's even taller than I thought.'

'Who?' I asked.

'The crown princess, of course!' Silke turned back to me just long enough to roll her eyes. 'Really, Aventurine, even you must have heard of her, no matter where you came from. Not only is she beautiful, she also speaks at least seven languages fluently *and* she's the finest diplomat the royal family's produced in the last two hundred years. *Everyone* loves her. She's going to be the best queen that we've ever had!'

'She sounds absolutely perfect,' I said sourly.

I knew all about older sisters like that.

I had far more sympathy, when I peered through the

glass, for the younger girl who was sitting at their table. Her skin was the same light brown as her older sister's, and her thick dark hair was arranged just as carefully, but her expression couldn't have been more different. Her older sister smiled serenely and carried on a flow of conversation with their pink-skinned, thickly set blond father as more and more faces pressed up against the front window of the shop. Neither of them seemed aware of the crowd gathering outside, or of the other customers whispering and staring in at them. The younger sister, though, had her shoulders hunched and her face squeezed into an expression of miserable discomfort. As I watched, her fingers rattled out a nervous rhythm against the table ... until her older sister reached out, still smiling as graciously as ever, and firmly pressed them into stillness.

Oh yes. I knew older sisters like that *much* too well.

And none of them was wearing a single crown. Not even the 'crown' princess.

So much for human royalty.

Sighing, I stepped away and let Horst hang the plate back in place, covering up the peephole. He was beaming as he stepped away ... until he caught sight of Marina.

'What are you doing?'

Marina's eyes narrowed as she poured the last of the chocolate creams into a glass. 'What does it look like I'm doing, Horst? Even you should recognise a few kitchen tricks by now.'

'But ...' He shook his head, wide-eyed. 'Did you not hear a word I said? The royal family –'

'Wants hot chocolates,' Marina finished for him. She arranged the eight chocolate creams neatly on to a tray, then tilted her head, considered them and began to shift the glasses around into different positions, like birds changing formation in a flock. 'I'm aware of that. And I'll get to them ... when I'm ready.'

Horst grabbed his hair with both hands. 'Are you *insane?*'

Silke's eyes widened. 'Er ... you might want to keep your voices down. I'm pretty sure the wall isn't *that* thick.'

'That's right.' Marina gave the glasses of chocolate cream a tight smile. 'We wouldn't want to scare the customers, would we?' She circled one glass of chocolate cream slowly around its tray, narrowed her eyes and reached for another.

'You – !' Horst reached out and grabbed the tray.

Marina grabbed the other end. Glasses clattered against each other in their struggle.

'Watch out,' she said, her grin turning feral. 'If any of these spill, I'll have to make them all over again. Then the royals would *really* have a long wait, wouldn't they?'

'What is wrong with you?' Horst demanded. He stepped back, panting hard. 'Don't you realise that we finally have the opportunity we've been dreaming of ? We could turn everything around after all! If the royals like your chocolate – if every paper in town reports that they came here and drank your hot chocolate and approved – !'

Taut lines formed around Marina's mouth. 'I don't care if the royals like my chocolate,' she said. 'That's not what I make it for.'

'That's not ... that's not – argh!' Horst slammed his fist against the wall, making the decorative plate rattle.

I ignored him. I'd been getting better at reading human expressions, especially Marina's, but there was something in her face now that I'd never seen before. I looked harder, trying to figure it out.

'Do you have *any idea* how close we're running to bankruptcy?' Horst glared at the wall that he'd just hit. 'If we don't find enough new customers soon – if our prima donna chocolatier doesn't throw a fit and scare away our final chance at survival –'

'Oh, *enough!*' Marina snarled. 'It's always about me ruining things, isn't it? It's all *my* fault the business is failing, according to you. It's all my fault that no one ever comes here. Never mind the fact that I'm only supposed to have to deal with the chocolate, I'm not *supposed* to be the one who deals with the public, or –' Her voice shook on the final syllable, and she slammed her mouth shut.

I'd never seen my mentor show such weakness before. I took a quick step closer, ready to protect her while she healed that telltale break in her scales.

'It's going to be all right,' I told her. 'You –'

'Don't worry about *her*, Aventurine,' Horst snapped. 'She's just throwing tantrums and trying to prove she's more important than royalty. Well, let me tell you something, Marina!' He bared his teeth at her. 'You're *not.*'

'Then that makes everything easier, doesn't it?' Marina snarled back. 'Because in that case, you won't mind when I walk out!' Reaching behind her neck, she unfastened her apron in one quick move and pulled it over her head. 'See? I'm finished. So you can find someone else to blame when this all goes wrong. Because I'm *not* going to be the one who ruins our final chance. Not this time!' And with that she threw the apron directly into Horst's face.

'Marina!' he growled, his voice muffled under the apron.

But she was already marching out through the door that led to the stairs and her own private quarters above the shop.

Horst yanked the apron off his face. 'Arrgh!' Looking murderous, he turned and lunged after Marina through the private door.

'But – !' Silke began, starting forward.

The door slammed closed. I could hear the thunder of feet running up the stairs.

Silke stared at the door, and then at me. She looked as stunned as if a hurricane had just blown past.

I sighed and added long silver spoons to the tray with the chocolate creams. 'Well, they won't be back for a while.'

Marina and Horst's everyday battles were bad enough, but this one ... They could take hours of shouting to resolve it.

Silke's eyes looked wild. 'But what about the *royal family*? They're still waiting for their hot chocolates. *With my handbill!*'

I looked at Silke, standing with me in the bright white kitchen in her bright red jacket and black trousers, with no chocolatier, no waiter and no authority in sight.

'So, these royals are really important,' I said, to make certain, 'even though they're not wearing crowns?'

'Yes!' Silke threw her hands in the air. 'So if you still want to save this chocolate house, despite the fact that it's run by people without a single shred of business sense between them ... !'

I would have glared at her for that, under normal circumstances. Right now, though, I had more important things to worry about.

I had a hoard to protect, and no one else to help me.

'All right,' I said. I took a deep breath. 'Then we'd better get started.'

CHAPTER 14

I had watched Marina make hot chocolates time and time again. But it felt more than intimidating to pick out one of her clean copper kettles for myself. It felt *wrong*. I had to stop myself from taking a guilty look backwards as I crossed the kitchen to the wall where they hung, to make sure she wasn't watching me do it.

I had never been allowed to make hot chocolate by myself, not even under Marina's supervision. I'd only watched, carefully taking note of every movement I could glimpse from my side of the kitchen, as she'd performed the all-important ritual.

'I hope you know how to do this,' Silke said, 'because if the royals don't like your hot chocolate, then everyone in this city will know it in less than an hour, and my brilliant handbill campaign will have been wasted. You'll never get a customer again ... and I'll never get my payment! Do you have any idea how many favours I had to call in, just to get that handbill printed in the first place?'

I gritted my teeth and grabbed the largest copper kettle. 'I'll be fine,' I told her. 'But you'd better get started.'

'What?' Her eyebrows shot upward. 'I don't know how to make chocolate! I can't –'

'Not that.' I pointed to the tray of chocolate creams. 'Those need to go out before they cool.'

'And you want me to deal with them?' Silke looked from the tray to me. Then she let out a crack of laughter. 'Oh, well,' she said. 'Why not? At least it'll be a new experience for all of us.' She gave a twirl, the tails of her red jacket flaring around her. 'I'll bet none of your fancy customers has ever been served by a girl like me before!'

Whistling through her teeth, she scooped up the tray and strode out through the swinging doors, her head held high. A moment later I heard her voice ringing out through the front room, strong and confident:

'Ladies and gentlemen! I believe some of you are waiting for these?'

Phew. She was gone. My shoulders relaxed. The last thing I needed was an audience as I tried to do this myself for the first time.

But when I tried to move forward, I couldn't do it. The kitchen suddenly seemed huge and echoingly empty. I could almost feel the walls expanding around me as I grew smaller and smaller, my chest tightening more with every moment. Too-familiar words suddenly rolled through my memory.

'Your scales haven't hardened enough to withstand even a wolf's bite ...'

'You may think yourself a ferocious beast, but outside this mountain you wouldn't survive a day ...'

I'd set out from my family's mountain twelve days ago to prove I really was capable of defending myself and our hoard, no matter what my mother claimed. But the Chocolate Heart wasn't just my personal hoard to defend. It was my final chance at happiness, too. If I made a single mistake now ...

'What are you waiting for, girl?' That was Marina's voice, sharp and strong in my memory. I squared my shoulders and stepped up to the cupboard where the round cakes of cooking chocolate were kept.

One dense, crumbly cake of chocolate, two round spoonfuls of ground sugar, water, milk ... a touch of cinnamon, a taste of vanilla, a breath of cloves, and for the final touch ... I paused, my hand hovering above the plate of fiery red chilli powder.

Marina had never told me exactly how much chilli she used in her chocolate.

Too much, and the royals would gasp and choke for breath. Too little, and the hot chocolate would be as bland as grass.

If I let myself wait and wonder any longer, I would never make a choice at all.

So I tossed a solid pinch of dried chilli pepper into the kettle before I could think any more about it. Either it would be perfect, or it would burn their mouths to cinders. I wouldn't know until they drank it.

Please, please, let this taste right! Let me save my hoard today. Let them love this place as much as I do!

The lid of the kettle rattled in my shaking fingers as I closed it and set the hot chocolate mix on to the charcoal brazier to cook.

Silke sailed back into the kitchen, her tray full of empty cups and glasses. '*Lots* more orders,' she said cheerfully. 'No one wants to leave while the royals are still here to gawp at. So at least you'll make plenty of silver for the chocolate house today ... even if your hot chocolate does turn out to be disgusting, eh?' She slid me a mischievous look.

But I couldn't even bring myself to rise to her bait. I had too much experimenting to do ... and *quickly*.

Chocolate creams, at least, I knew how to make. I had no idea how to make the pastry for chocolate tarts, but luckily, a dozen pastry shells sat waiting in their baking dishes on the counter, prepared by Marina earlier that morning. I mixed together a big bowl of fresh, eggy chocolate filling for the tarts, and as I poured out the rich, sweet-smelling mixture into all of the little pastry-lined baking dishes, I hoped with all my heart that they would taste as good once they were baked as they smelt at that moment.

But nothing else mattered as much as the royals' hot chocolates. As soon as the kettle was ready, I shoved the tarts into the oven and abandoned everything else to pour the steaming liquid into the three most elegant silver chocolate pots we owned, while Silke hovered over my shoulder. Then I growled until she moved away so that I could use the long wooden molinet to froth the hot chocolates, one by one. I could feel the clock ticking steadily away in the front room, while the royal family – and their watchers – waited for their service ... but just as Marina had instructed me the very first time we'd met, I took my time with every one of them, not stinting so much as an instant of care.

My hot chocolates had to be absolutely perfect. They had to be so good, the royals would *want* to save the Chocolate Heart, for all of our sakes.

Finally, I set all three hot-chocolate pots in a row on a tray, along with three beautifully ornamented porcelain cups in silver cases.

'At least they look pretty,' Silke said. 'So, now we'll see, eh?' Dropping me a wink, she picked up the tray. 'Feel free to watch through that little peephole as I have my one and only interaction with royalty! I'll need a witness if I want my brother to believe me when I tell him what I did today.'

I yanked the decorative plate off the wall as the kitchen doors swung shut behind her.

There were more and more people crowding outside the Chocolate Heart now, pushing and shoving for position in front of the broad glass windows. For the first time since I'd moved into the chocolate house, every single table was occupied, and a long line had formed at the front door.

Silke was right. If the king took one sip and gagged – or coughed, or winced and set the cup aside – *everyone* would know about it. And I was beginning to understand humans by now. It didn't matter how many people had tasted Marina's hot chocolate before and loved it. If any of them heard that the royal family hadn't liked it, they would immediately decide that they didn't either.

Humans really were herd animals. And now I was at their mercy.

Silke swept up to the royal table as if she'd been mixing with the upper crust her whole life, smiling and chatting as she laid down the tray. The king was so lost in thought he didn't even seem to notice, his eyes narrowed and his gaze fixed on his hands, which were clasped together on the table in front of him. The crown princess gave Silke a smile, though, and said something that made Silke's own smile deepen. At the sight of the three chocolate pots, even the youngest princess straightened, looking suddenly hopeful. She started to reach for hers, and I tensed, waiting ... but then her older sister gave a tiny head-shake and she subsided, looking embarrassed.

Silke poured for each of them with a flourish. Then she scooped up the empty tray and moved back a step, looking expectant.

I waited with her, holding my breath.

The crown princess looked at her father. Nothing happened. His gaze was still fixed on his hands. The younger princess reached out again for her own cup, but she snatched back her hand at a stern look from her older sister.

Not a single customer in the whole shop was moving. Every gaze was fixed on their table.

Then the king gave a sudden start, his eyes flying wide open. The crown princess smiled and nodded towards his cup.

Grimacing, he nodded. He reached out, lifted the cup to his lips ...

And the front door of the chocolate house flew open. The small, perpetually annoyed-looking man who'd run his fingers over the paintwork in our front room four days earlier marched inside, along with the tall, brown-haired woman who had tried to bribe me. At the sight of her wide, satisfied smile, everything inside me braced for danger.

'Attention!' the man bellowed. 'By order of the lord mayor himself, all customers are hereby required to vacate this chocolate house immediately. We are here to inspect this establishment!'

I slammed my way through the swinging doors into the front room just as half the customers in the chocolate house jumped to their feet, blocking my way. Voices rose around the room, calling out in confusion and outrage, but they all fell silent as one man spoke:

'My good man.' It was the king; when I stood on tiptoes and peered between the two men in front of me, I could see him still sitting at his table, looking astonishingly calm. 'May I ask why, exactly, these premises need so urgently to be inspected?'

'They – ungh!' The lord mayor's man turned pale as his gaze fell on the king and the two princesses. He stumbled into a bow. 'Your Maj–'

The crown princess cleared her throat meaningfully.

The king shook his head.

Silke said, 'May I present Count von Reimann, a *valued customer* of this establishment?'

'Sir!' The lord mayor's man straightened, looking panicked. 'We didn't expect to see – that is – the lord mayor wants – but –'

'Perhaps,' said Silke, 'you could wait just a few more minutes to carry out your important inspection? After all, don't you think the lord mayor would prefer *Count von Reimann* to be allowed to enjoy his drink first?'

'Well ...' His eyes darted from side to side as the king watched him smilingly, one regal hand already resting on the royal chocolate cup. Next to the king, the younger princess reached for her own cup with a hopeful look, and the lord mayor's man sighed. 'Perhaps ... oh ... I'm sure he wouldn't really mind ...'

'Ahem.' His colleague elbowed him aside. Her gaze swept the room, her lips twitching as she met my eyes through the press of bodies. 'The lord mayor,' she announced, in a voice more than loud enough to reach every onlooker peering through the glass outside, 'has received deeply, *deeply* disturbing reports of the serious lack of hygiene in this establishment, accounts so troubling they must be resolved without delay for the sake of every person in this building. After all, if there truly are rats running around the kitchen floors ... cockroaches in the cupboard where the chocolate is kept ... massive patches of creeping mould beside the ovens ... and old hot chocolates left out for days, only to be reheated again and again for each new customer who comes – !'

Cries of horror erupted throughout the room, drowning out her voice as she continued her recitation.

But I didn't need to hear the rest of her words. I was already shoving my way through the crowd, pushing grown customers aside and growling fiercely as all the fear I'd felt earlier drained out of me. If I'd had my claws, I would have ripped her into shreds before she could speak another poisonous word! I was more than ready to take on this territorial challenge.

'Those are lies!' I was panting with effort by the time I reached the royal table, where the king and both princesses were rising to their feet, leaving their hot chocolates completely untouched. The older royals were back to looking cool and expressionless, but the younger princess's face was twisted up in disgust, and she'd shoved her hot-chocolate cup as far from her seat as possible. 'She's making all of this up!' I told them. 'The lord mayor hates us. He's been trying to shut us down for ages. He –'

'Well, I suppose we know now why no one's ever allowed into the kitchens.' The king sighed. 'Pity. I should have liked to meet a real food mage, just once. They're supposed to be rather quirky and entertaining chaps, not like all those grim battle mages who can't stop groaning on and on about dragons. Never mind. Shall we ... ?'

He tilted his head at the front door, where eight different people were all trying to squeeze their way out at once. One man was gibbering loudly about rats, while his female companion held her parasol like a weapon, just waiting to stab some imaginary vermin in self-defence.

'No!' I said. 'Just listen to me. This is ridiculous. It's a trick! It's –'

'Leaving now, before things get even messier, would certainly be sensible.' The lord mayor's woman gave the king a smile as sweet as sugar.

I burned for the ability to shoot flame. 'You can look at the kitchens right now,' I said desperately. 'All of you! Come with me, and you'll see for yourself. There's no mould! There aren't any rats or cockroaches! There's –'

'Would you like a tour?' Silke asked, gesturing towards the kitchen doors. 'We'd be more than happy and honoured to show you –'

'A tour?' The lord mayor's woman laughed. 'How exactly are we meant to have any tour without the presence or authority of the infamous head chocolatier? She's not coming out even for this, is she?' She turned to the king. 'Are you really going to ignore the decision of the lord mayor on the say-so of two children you don't even know? A waitress wearing scandalous boys' clothing, and a disreputable apprentice already known to be violent?'

Her voice half dropped, as if she was sharing secrets, as she looked straight at me. 'I know all about this girl, you see. She was thrown bodily from the doors of every respectable chocolate house in town, because she came

138

from the streets. So trust me, sir: you can't take her word on anything.'

That was it. I'd had enough of human diplomacy. This was war!

I flew at her, snarling, with my hands outstretched.

Silke's arms clamped around my waist just before my fingernails could rake the woman's face like claws. 'No!' she hissed. 'Aventurine, *think*!'

'You see?' The lord mayor's woman was breathing quickly as she pointed at me. 'This girl is positively feral! Do you want an animal like that making your chocolate?'

I writhed in Silke's grip, glaring at the lord mayor's woman. If she wanted to see what an animal would do, I was more than ready to oblige her. 'You – !'

'Young lady ...' The crown princess startled me into silence by stepping forward and putting her cool hands lightly around mine. 'I do admire your loyalty,' she told me, 'and I appreciate your offer to see this mysterious kitchen for ourselves. However –' she gave me a steady look – 'the cafes and restaurants of Drachenburg follow the laws of the lord mayor and his town council, and neither of them has requested our assistance here. After all –' she gave me a rueful half-smile – 'we are only a count and his daughters, at least for today. You see?'

'No!' I said. 'I don't!'

She squeezed my hands gently and then let go, shaking her head, as her father and sister started for the front door. 'I do wish you all the best of luck in the future.'

'I don't need help *later*.' I was almost choking with frustration. 'I need it *now*. You have to listen to me! Wait!'

But the crown princess was already turning her warm, sympathetic smile to the lord mayor's two assistants. 'And I wish *you* both good fortune in the performance of your civic duties.'

'We thank you, my lady.' The lord mayor's woman ducked her head as she lowered herself into an elaborate curtsy. Still, I could see her grin, not even half hidden, and it made my stomach roil.

As the crown princess followed her father out of the chocolate shop, ignoring all of my last, desperately shouted protests, the bell over the door sounded a maliciously bright jingle ... and bile ran down my throat, as bitter and scorching as my lost flame.

This can't be happening!

But it was.

I had set out to prove myself when I left my family's mountain.

But – just as my own mother had predicted – I had failed.

My roar of despair echoed through the abandoned room.

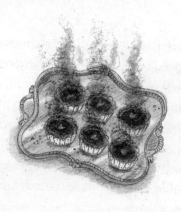

CHAPTER 15

Less than ten minutes after I had made my first hot chocolate, the once-busy, bustling Chocolate Heart was empty. Not a single onlooker had lingered outside after the royal family departed with the rest of the customers. Even the lord mayor's woman spent scarcely two minutes longer in the chocolate house, while her colleague popped his head into the kitchen but didn't bother to step all the way inside.

'Looks fine to me,' he called back.

'Well, what a marvellous relief.' The lord mayor's woman gave us a vicious smile as she wrote out the certificate of inspection. She laid it on the closest table with a flourish. 'What a triumph for you all to have had those terrible rumours disproved. I'll be certain to pass on your deepest thanks to the lord mayor.'

Silke's hand tightened on my shoulder, but it didn't need to. I only bared my teeth at the woman's taunts. I didn't even have it in me to snarl.

I would have buried myself underneath the furthest mountain in the world if I could, and never shown my face in the outside air again. But at that moment I couldn't have lifted myself up out of my chair for the promise of a whole cavern-ful of gold.

I had lost the battle to defend my own territory. There was no greater humiliation for a dragon.

When the front door finally closed behind them with a *clink*, Silke let out a gusting breath. 'Phew!' She collapsed on to the chair across from me at the royal table, then leaned forward as something caught her eye. She lifted the closest cup, sniffed it and took a tiny sip. Her eyes widened. 'Well,' she said, 'it may not be hot any more, but it really is good chocolate.'

Laughter and rage bubbled up inside me until I could barely tell them apart.

I wanted to burn up the city with flames shooting straight from my no-longer-armoured throat. I wanted to rip the world apart with the claws I didn't have.

As Silke took another, longer sip, the kitchen doors swung open behind me. Horst's voice came out as an anguished gasp. 'What in heaven's name has *happened* here?'

My heart sank. With a massive, grinding effort, I turned my head.

Marina stood behind Horst, her arms crossed and her face perfectly blank. Her gaze moved slowly across the empty tables ... and, finally, landed on me, sitting at the royal table with the three best chocolate cups and pots all laid out in front of me.

Suddenly, I could barely breathe.

I'd seen that disappointment in my mother's eyes before. But I'd never, ever seen it from Marina.

Silke gave a laugh that grated against my ears. 'Good news,' she said wryly, and held up the certificate. 'You've passed the lord mayor's inspection for cleanliness!'

'His ... *what*?' Horst shook his head, his face looking almost gaunt with panic. 'We were gone for less than twenty minutes,' he said. 'What could possibly have gone so badly wrong in that short time?'

Silke snorted, lifting the chocolate cup to her lips and settling back against her chair. 'Oh, do you want the full story? Or just the highlights? Which do you think would be better, Aventurine?'

'Yes, Aventurine.' For the first time Marina spoke, her voice flat and hard. 'Why don't *you* tell us the story, please?'

Her words made every inch of my back clench.

I knew that tone of voice. How could I not? I'd heard it from my mother a hundred times before, as she prepared to find out exactly what I'd done wrong ... again.

Mother had warned me that I wasn't as strong as I thought I was. She would have been horrified at the idea of leaving me to fight such an important battle for the chocolate house alone. She would never have trusted me to do it.

Marina's head jerked around. 'Wait a minute. What's

that burning smell?' Without waiting for an answer, she lunged back through the swinging doors into the kitchen.

The kitchen ...

Oh no. The chocolate tarts! I'd left them in the oven when I went charging out to confront the lord mayor's woman.

How could I have forgotten them?

Horror rooted me to my seat as Horst hurried after her, the doors swinging shut behind him. Marina's bellow sounded a moment later. 'Just look at this mess! They're ruined!'

'Uh-oh,' Silke said, and hopped up out of her seat. 'Better go and take a look ...'

But I couldn't look at the mess I'd created. I couldn't do anything but sit, frozen in my seat, as Silke hurried after the others and voices rose beyond the swinging doors.

What was the first thing Marina had ever said about me to Horst? *'No one important will be offended when I toss her out on her ear for being useless.'*

I'd failed to defend the Chocolate Heart from attack ... and now I'd failed as a chocolatier, too. How much more useless could any apprentice be? The sound that escaped my lips, as I realised that, wasn't a word in any language. It wasn't even a moan. It was a sound of pain that came straight from my gut, and it made my decision for me even before I saw the kitchen doors begin to swing open.

'Aventurine!' Marina bellowed.

I'd thought that I couldn't move, but I'd been wrong. I ran out of the Chocolate Heart as if the worst predators on earth were closing in behind me ... and I had become the most cowardly of prey.

Dragons never ran away. I knew that. Dragons always stood and fought, no matter how bad the odds might be. But my family had been right about me after all.

I wasn't strong, fierce or patient enough to be trusted in the world outside.

From the lessons that I'd ignored in my family's cavern, to the moment when I'd fallen for that scoundrelly food mage's trick, I had failed in everything important that I'd tried. Now I'd failed in my own passion, too: the one thing I was supposed to be best at. The only thing that I'd had left. And as soon as I stopped running, I would have to face what that meant ...

So I didn't stop running. I couldn't make myself stop, even when my chest started burning and my side felt as if a claw had slid inside it and was turning back and forth, skewering me with every movement.

I didn't stop even after the tears on my face had all been blown away by the cold wind that slapped against my cheeks.

Running away wasn't brave, and it wasn't fierce. But it had to be better than sitting and waiting to be tossed out. I couldn't bear to have that happen again. Not this time. Not by Marina. Not from the only chocolate house in Drachenburg that had given me a chance ... and from the only family that I'd had left, after I had lost my first one forever.

A gurgling sound of pain escaped me and I doubled over, gasping for breath and grabbing my legs through my dress.

There were people moving all around me, but I didn't care. They could think what they liked of me. I'd already lost my teeth and claws and family, and now I'd lost my chocolate, too – and every human I'd learned to care about would pay for my failure.

It didn't matter that the Chocolate Heart had passed its inspection. Right now, gossip would be racing all around the city, human after human excitedly passing on the news that the kitchen in the Chocolate Heart was so disgusting the lord mayor had been forced to shut it down. I wouldn't be surprised if, by tomorrow, every potential customer in town had heard what the king had said about it, too: '*I suppose we know now why no one's ever allowed into the kitchens ...*'

None of them would ever hear what the actual results of the inspection had been ... and none of them would ever care enough to find out.

And I hadn't even –

'Aventurine?' A woman's voice gasped my name. 'Oh my goodness. It *is* you! I can hardly believe it!'

I turned my head. A forest-green skirt swished beside me. Dark green shoes peeked out from underneath.

I wouldn't have bothered to look up to find out more, but the skirt suddenly rustled and its owner knelt down beside me, beaming and balancing a market basket on her knees. 'It's me, you silly girl! *Greta!*'

Oh. Greta. In all the excitement of the last week and a half, I'd nearly forgotten about her and her ridiculous abduction attempt. I certainly didn't have time for her now.

Sighing, I looked back down. But I couldn't recapture my train of thought, not with her chattering only inches from my ears, her pale round face turning pink with excitement.

'I am *so* glad to see you alive, you wouldn't believe it. Oh, the nightmares I've had of you falling into the river! Or being set upon by thieves, or ...'

Slowly, disbelievingly, I turned my head. 'How could I have fallen into the river?' I asked. 'It's surrounded by banks, and all the bridges have rails.'

'Well, I don't know. You might not have noticed it and just walked in.'

I stared at her.

'Well, you're not from around here, are you? You don't know how big cities work, or what to do. And it was our responsibility to look after you, you know, since you would never have survived without us in the first place.' Setting down her basket, which was full of fresh fruit and vegetables, Greta heaved a sigh that ruffled my hair. 'Oh, if I've said it to Friedrich once, I've said it a hundred times ... I've never seen any girl less capable of looking after herself than you.'

That did it. I let go of my legs and straightened to my full height. It wasn't hard to breathe after all, or to summon up a good glare for the woman in front of me. 'Goodbye,' I said as icily as Marina ever could, and I turned to leave.

'No, wait!' She jumped up and grabbed my arm. 'Just look at you! That dress is hideous –'

'Stones and bones!' After two weeks of grinding cocoa nibs, it was easy to yank my arm free from her grip. 'Why doesn't anyone ever like my dress?'

'*And* you look like you've been crying,' Greta added.

Humiliation froze me in place. I tightened my jaw and ground my words through my teeth: 'That was just the wind against my face.'

'Oh, really?' She put her hands on her hips. 'Then why, exactly, do you look so miserable?'

Me?

I tried to laugh a barking, contemptuous laugh at the idea.

The noise that came out of my mouth sounded horribly like a sob.

I slammed my lips shut, but it was too late.

'I knew it!' Greta said. 'I just knew you couldn't make it on your own in this city – a wild, careless, ignorant girl like you.' She shook her head. 'Well, how could you? You're only a child, and you didn't know a single soul here, except for us. You don't know how to behave or even how to dress. Just look at your eyes – they're like an animal's! Now look at what a mess you've made of yourself. Your hair – your clothes – !' She waved her hand at my glorious purple-and-gold dress. 'No one wears colours like that together!'

Well, that part might actually have been true. I'd certainly never seen anyone else in Drachenburg dressed quite like me.

Usually, I liked that. But today it made a creeping, cold feeling trickle over my shoulder blades. Would the crown princess have taken me more seriously if I'd been dressed more like everyone else?

Greta *tske*'d between her teeth as she looked at me. 'And you really thought *you* could go to work in a chocolate house? As if any of those fine places would ever let you through their doors!'

I ground my teeth together as I glared back at her, the words burning in my throat: *they did!*

For one brief, beautiful moment, I'd had everything I needed. I'd had my passion. I'd been surrounded by chocolate. I'd had a new home and a hoard, and I'd had Marina, too.

But as I looked into Greta's pitying face, I remembered the smell of burning tarts and I knew she was right – just like my family had been right about me, too. I had been given everything I could want in my new body, and I had lost it all through my own unforgivable weakness.

I thought about the expression on Marina's face when she had seen me sitting at the abandoned royal table ... and at that memory, the final tiny breath of flame inside me flickered and died out.

That was what happened when I tried to look after important things myself.

Greta must have seen the defeat in my slumped shoulders.

'Oh dear.' Sighing, she patted my arm and reached down for her basket. 'I know you're a good girl really, at heart. Now, why don't you just take this for me? *That* shouldn't require any manners or common sense, so even you should be able to manage it, dear. And at least you're strong, so that's something. We'll go home and have a nice cup of tea, and then I'll start showing you how to do everything around the house. We already have a room waiting for you, you know – I just knew, somehow, that you'd come back in the end! Because, really, where else could you go?'

She smiled as she hooked the heavy basket around my unresisting arm. 'Oh, don't look so sad, Aventurine. I promise you'll feel at home with us in no time! Soon you won't even remember this past week and a half. It'll be as if it never even happened!'

Smoke would have billowed up my throat at that, in the old days. But I had lost the right to defend myself today ... and Greta wasn't wrong after all.

I had nowhere else to go.

So I followed her down the road, my throat as hard as a column of un-ground sugar, and I felt the truth all through my body.

I didn't deserve to call myself a dragon any more.

CHAPTER 16

At least being an unpaid maid was easy. All it took was shutting off my brain and my heart so I could do everything Greta wanted without letting myself think or feel anything at all.

I was good at following orders, after eleven days in Marina's kitchen. I was strong enough that hard work didn't bother me.

And the last thing I wanted was to let my brain or my heart take control of me ever again.

It was impossible to shut them off completely, though. At night, when I lay in the soft, sagging bed that Greta had given me, in my tiny, claustrophobic pink bedroom, with the rose-painted walls pressing in around me and the piled quilts doing their best to smother me, the remembered scent of roasting cocoa beans felt like a ghost in the room. I would grit my teeth and close my eyes, but I couldn't forget that smell, or the feeling of rightness it had carried.

I still dreamed of running through endless dark and empty tunnels in my family's mountain every night. But now my family's voices weren't the only ones I heard calling out to me. Marina's voice sounded, too, firm and impatient, summoning me to my next task and setting me alight with hope ... then disappearing, every time.

At every new turn in the tunnel, the scent of chocolate taunted me. But I could never, ever recapture its taste.

In the mornings I woke with my quilts kicked on to the floor and sweat trickling down my neck, no matter how chilly the room around me. My stomach felt as hollow as an empty shell, and the longing for my scale-cloth ached all through my bones.

Marina had probably tossed it out by now, just as she would have tossed me out if I'd stayed any longer. But I wished I'd taken the time to save my scale-cloth before I'd left. I might not be a dragon any more, but I was terribly, coldly afraid that without the pattern of my old scales to remind me, I would lose even the memory of flame. And then ...

No.

Thoughts like that sent me leaping out of bed every morning, slamming a lid on my emotions the way I might have clamped a lid on a pot, until not even the tiniest shred of steam could escape into the air. After I'd woken to thoughts and feelings like that, it felt only right to spend the rest of the morning torturing myself with endless floor-scrubbing or dealing with chamber pots worse than I could ever have imagined.

Once, Friedrich tried to quietly offer me some money for the work I was doing, but Greta came into the room and caught him at it. Those coins went directly into her purse, and she lectured him for the next five minutes about his irresponsible, spendthrift nature. From then on he just avoided my eyes whenever he came across me.

But the truth was, I didn't mind not being paid. What would I have used the money for anyway? In the human world, money was to be spent in shops, not slept on ... and the last thing I wanted was to ever step out into the wider world again.

On my third full day of service, though, Greta forced me out of the house.

'Come along,' she said brightly as I finished the last of the chamber pots. 'I'll show you everything we need at the market, so you can take over the shopping, too.'

'The river market?' I was so horrified I accidentally let myself breathe in the rancid stench from the chamber pot I was cleaning. It made me gag, but it wasn't nearly as bad as the thought of running into Silke. Having her see me like this – !

I shuddered.

So did Greta. 'You think I would ever dream of setting foot at the *river* market?' she demanded. 'No respectable woman would ever shop there! Those ruffians sleep in tents out by their tables, did you know that? Right there on the mud, and who knows where they come from? I wouldn't trust them for an instant! No, I'm talking about the *proper* market.'

Oh. My shoulders relaxed and I bent back over my disgusting chore.

At least Greta's market sounded boring enough to be safe.

When we stepped outside ten minutes later, though, I sucked in my breath as if a scab had just been pulled off from my skin. The sun felt too bright. There were shifting colours everywhere and people filling the street with their chatter and their movement. Smells floated down the street from every direction, and the air tasted frighteningly fresh, crisp and cold and full of possibilities that didn't belong to me. Not any more.

I backed towards the doorway, still holding the market basket along with Greta's shopping list. 'Maybe I should stay here and –'

'Don't be silly,' Greta snapped, and started off ahead of me. 'You look perfectly respectable nowadays. Now that I can trust you to behave sensibly, there's no reason you shouldn't be the one who does the shopping from now on. It'll give me time to get some proper sewing done, for once! Friedrich needs new carpet slippers, you know, and I'm sick to death of our old tablecloth. I want to embroider a new one, to show all the ladies who visit me. And there are at least a dozen social calls I should have made by now that I put off just to help you settle in, so really, the least you could do is help me, too. Hurry *up*, Aventurine!'

I did. I was wearing a loose, drab, mud-brown dress that had belonged to Greta's last maid, as well as an even darker brown bonnet that hid my hair. With the market basket in my hand, I blended in exactly with the stream of other humans on the street. Even the sharpest-eyed predator flying overhead could never have picked me out of the herd.

So there was no reason at all for me to feel more alone than I ever had before.

By the time we'd reached the market, though, my skin had finally settled back into itself, after the first rawness of exposure to the outside world. At least no one was likely to be watching me now, and there was no one here who knew about my humiliation. Marina got all of her supplies from a big spice-scented market hall that catered only to the restaurants and cafes in town. And the market that Greta led me to now, in the bright, shiny centre of the second district, was a world away from the slippery, sucking mud of the riverbank where Silke's brother worked. There was no one who knew me in this crowded open square full of polished wooden stalls and bustling women in busy groups, all arguing over the finest fabrics and the freshest vegetables for their families.

All I had to do was trot after Greta and hold her basket as it grew heavier and heavier around my arm ... and try not to listen to the whispers surging all around me.

'... My cousin said in his last letter that he saw two of those monsters flying together, not ten miles from his farm! He said they flew back and forth for hours.'

'Horrible creatures! Those battle mages ought to march out to the mountains and take care of them before they can do any real damage. That's what I think!'

'Oh, absolutely. Exterminate them like the vermin they are!'

Don't think about it, I chanted to myself. *Just don't think!*

I gritted my blunt human teeth and cleared my head until I could think of nothing, nothing at all ... not even when I spotted a flock of black-robed battle mages ahead, striding self-importantly through the crowd and leaving an awestruck wake behind them.

My family would eat those stupid battle mages if they tried anything ... and there was nothing I could do about it anyway.

But what was happening in my family's mountain without me?

Five minutes later Greta caught sight of someone over my head. 'Oh. O*h!* I can hardly believe it!' She lifted herself up on tiptoe to wave across the crowd. 'Aventurine, I'm going to leave you to do the rest of the shopping yourself. I don't know how on earth she's managed it, but – well, that's one of my *oldest* friends, and believe it or not, she's walking arm in arm with a cousin of the lord mayor himself! I *have* to go and say hello. Maybe we can even take tea together!'

My mouth had gone dry at the words 'the lord mayor'.

'I don't want –'

'Oh no, don't worry, *you* don't have to come along,' Greta said. 'Trust me, no one wants to meet my maid!' She let out a high trill of laughter. 'I hope you didn't think that I'd be buying tea for you! No, I'm going to teach you how to make it yourself, once I trust that you *might* be ready. I'm sure, with a little practice, you'll learn to be competent enough – at least when no one important is around to taste it.'

How my tail would have lashed at that, if I'd still been a dragon! If she only knew everything that I'd learned and done in Marina's kitchen ...

But I remembered burned tarts, and my shoulders slumped. I accepted the coins that she counted out for me, and I set off alone, with the heavy wicker basket hanging over my arm, as Greta hurried towards her friend.

I was standing in line at a cheese stall a few minutes later when I felt something brush against my arm. I jerked away, slapping a protective hand against the hidden pocket in my dress where Greta's coins were kept ...

And then I recognised Silke's laughter.

'The look on your face!' she said. '*Thieves beware.* I see she's finally let you out of your prison?'

'*What?*' I jerked around as the line shuffled forward without me.

It was utterly bizarre to see Silke standing here in Greta's market square: my old life had suddenly been transplanted into my new one, and the two didn't fit together at all. I felt dizzy at the sight of her, so close and so real, making the memory of the last few days feel almost dreamlike. She stood with her thumbs planted in her pockets, watching me keenly through her clever dark eyes and wearing a green jacket and trousers that might have actually looked conservative ... if only she was a boy.

'How did you find me?' I demanded.

Silke shrugged, bouncing on her heels. 'I knew she'd have to let you out at some point. When I saw the two of you setting off today with a market basket, it wasn't exactly difficult to guess the rest.'

'But ...' I stopped, biting my tongue.

Silke's smirk intensified, though, just as if I'd let the rest of my foolish question escape. 'Didn't you realise? I can figure out anything that's going on in this city. I've known where you were for over a day now; I just hadn't worked out a way in yet.'

'But why were you even trying?' I asked.

Silke blinked. Her smile slipped. 'Sorry?'

I shook my head impatiently and moved out of the line, forcing her back so that I could get safely away from the women waiting behind me. I couldn't bear for this conversation to be repeated back to Greta.

We were a full three feet away and hidden in the shifting crowd before I hissed, 'Why were you looking for me in the first place? If you're still hunting for your payment, you must know I can't get it for you.' My stomach soured as I imagined it. 'Horst and Marina won't care what I say. Not any more.'

At my first words, Silke's face had gone completely blank. Now, though, her eyes narrowed. 'Is that what you really think?'

Well, I might not have been a dragon any more, but

that didn't mean I was completely pathetic ... and it was just stupid to roll over in front of a predator and show them your vulnerable underbelly. So I stuck my jaw out and didn't answer.

'Wherever it is that you come from, Aventurine,' said Silke, 'I think things must be done pretty strangely. Because I'm not pretending that money isn't important ... but around here, there's such a thing as friendship, too.'

My shoulders hunched. I eyed her warily, through slitted eyes, holding Greta's basket tight against my stomach.

I didn't need to be told that I wasn't Silke's friend after what had happened at the Chocolate Heart, ruining all the effects of her clever handbill. If she'd tracked me down just to tell me that, she had wasted her time.

I didn't need human friends anyway. I didn't need anyone.

She looked at me and sighed. 'Are you honestly telling me that you'd rather be a maid than an apprentice chocolatier?'

Now that really was a question too stupid to deserve an answer.

Silke said, 'How much is she paying you, anyway? Anything at all? Because the gossip I heard was that she's been bragging to all her friends about how clever she's been, getting a stupid country girl to be her servant and do all her dirty work for free.'

My teeth clenched, but I didn't answer.

'Fine.' Silke flung up her hands. 'I give in! You're clearly having a wonderful time in your new life. Scrubbing floors was probably what you were born to do. Who even likes the taste of chocolate anyway?' She tilted her head to one side, her eyes bright. 'But about that payment that you promised me all those days ago ...'

I unclamped my jaw just enough to grind out, 'I don't have enough money to pay you myself.'

'I know,' Silke said, with creamy satisfaction. 'So you'll have to do something different for me instead, won't you?' She jerked one thumb over her shoulder. 'Come with me. It'll only take you five minutes, and your new employer won't even notice. She's off fraternising with the lord mayor's cousin right now, sucking up with all her might. I saw them heading towards the most expensive tea room in this district, so they'll be gone for at least half an hour. Now's your chance to pay your debt in private and be all hers from then on, for evermore.'

I hesitated. Silke was definitely up to something.

'Come on!' Silke took another step backwards, beckoning for me to follow. 'Do you really want me harassing you for payment every time she sends you to the market from now on? This is your chance to be free! You'll never see me – or be reminded of your old apprenticeship – ever again. Just exactly the way you want it. Right?'

My stomach twisted in a sudden shock of pain, and I jerked my head down to hide my expression. 'Fine!' I said tightly. I adjusted my grip on the basket and started after her, keeping my head lowered and my emotions tightly compressed as we wove through the busy crowd.

I was working so hard not to feel, and not to think,

that it took me a moment to realise, a few minutes later, that Silke had finally come to a stop. I stumbled to a halt two steps past her and saw, with an uneasy lurch of my stomach, that she had a mischievous smirk on her face. We were outside the main bulk of the market by then, past the final wooden stall and not far from a big stone fountain with a statue in the middle. Bracing myself, I lifted my head and looked around, hunting for clues.

The crowd had thinned out, but there were still plenty of people on this side of the square. A street cook's oven stood ten feet away, producing hot crêpes that sent the sweet smells of sugar and cooking strawberries and bananas swirling into the fresh cold air. Pigeons pecked around the large colourful tiles on the ground, trilling and clucking as they chased after crumbs. People sat alone or in groups along the wide stone rim of the fountain, chatting to their friends and eating their crêpes ...

And in the middle of it all, alone and watching me from her seat on the rim of the fountain, sat Marina.

She crossed her arms.

'Hello, Aventurine.'

CHAPTER 17

Silke grabbed my arm before I could move.

She didn't have to. My whole body felt as if it had been turned to stone, just like the fountain where Marina sat. I couldn't have run away again even if I'd wanted to.

As I looked into Marina's steady gaze, though, I realised the truth: I had done enough running. For better or for worse, it was time to take what was coming to me.

Marina nodded to Silke, her expression grim. 'I'd like a few minutes alone with my apprentice, if you don't mind.'

'Absolutely.' Silke sketched a mock bow to Marina, gave me a nudge with one elbow and took off.

I didn't turn to watch her go.

'Sit down, Aventurine,' said Marina.

Slowly, I walked over to sit beside her. The stone rim

of the fountain was cold underneath me, the chill soaking through my thin dress, but I didn't complain.

I'd survived the fireball that my own grandfather had thrown at me, the day that I'd lost my first family. I could survive this, too.

She nodded to the basket that still hung over my arm. 'That for your new employer?'

I nodded without speaking or meeting her gaze.

'Hmm.' Out of the corner of my eye, I caught her studying my plain brown dress. 'You decided to go into hiding with your clothing, too?'

I jerked one shoulder in a shrug and forced my voice out past the choke in my throat. 'You told me my last dress was ugly.'

'That's because it looked like an exploded tin of paints,' she said. 'But at least it was an interesting explosion. You're not even trying to stand out any more?'

My face felt hot, despite the cold air, as I felt Marina's piercing gaze on me. I fought to keep my breathing steady, my chin up. I wasn't going to humiliate myself again, no matter what. I'd done enough of that already.

Finally, she let out a sigh and uncrossed her arms. 'All right. I'm going to tell you a story, Aventurine. But you'd better listen carefully, because I'll only tell it once. And I'm warning you right now: I don't want to hear you bring it up ever again.' She set one strong, gold-toned hand on the rim of the fountain beside me, and I saw her fingers whiten as she clenched the stone. 'I didn't grow up in Drachenburg, you know, any more than you did.'

I sneaked a glance at her. It was safe enough now; she wasn't looking at me any more. Instead she gazed broodingly ahead, her expression unfocused, as if she was seeing something completely different from the wooden market stalls and the pigeons pecking around in front of us. When she finally spoke again, her voice sounded muted, as if it was coming from far away.

'I wasn't so different from you, you know, back when I first started out. Mad for chocolate, from the moment I discovered it. I was meant to be a fisherman's wife; that's the life all the girls in my family were raised to. But I wouldn't have it.'

She shook her head slowly. 'After I tasted my first sample of chocolate, off one of the boats that came into our harbour, I walked all the way to the capital city. Then I moved on to Villenne, across the ocean, when I heard that the chocolatiers there were the best. See, I always wanted to be the best. So I worked and I found myself a place where I could learn. I was the youngest chocolatier in that city, you know – the only woman, too – and, oh, was I proud of it.' She snorted. 'Couldn't believe anything would ever go wrong. Didn't even think that was possible, no matter what I tried ... no matter who I offended ... no matter what I was challenged to do, with the whole world watching me do it. And then ...'

Her voice dropped to a low whisper. 'With the whole court and every rival I'd ever had all standing there, watching, in the final round of a national competition, I gave the queen of Villenne – the single person whose taste mattered most in the entire kingdom – a chocolate cream made with milk that had gone sour.' She took a shuddering breath. 'It was a fix, you see – someone had planted sour milk in my kitchen just in time for the competition, to pay me back for being rude to them. But I should have known. I should have tested it before I used it. For once, though, I didn't even bother to check.'

Her lips twisted. 'I was too busy planning out all the great things I'd do next, after I won. I'd won all of those competitions for so long, I thought it was a sure thing … right up until the queen put that spoon into her mouth. But the look on her face when she tasted that spoonful – then spat it out in front of everyone, because it was disgusting – !'

Marina closed her eyes for a moment, fresh lines popping up in her tightly pinched cheeks. Then she blew out her breath in a sigh. 'Well. Those fancy courtiers made a lot of jokes about my chocolate that night. The queen made one or two herself, and those ones got printed in the papers the next day. By the day after that, everyone in town was retelling all those jokes to each other, and pretty soon even the name of my chocolate house had become a joke. And I could tell you every other nasty detail of how it all came crashing down around me … but all that really matters is, I failed.'

Her eyes opened, but she kept her heavy gaze turned away from me. 'I failed in front of all the most influential people in that kingdom, but more importantly, I failed in front of myself. And right then I would have given anything to curl up and disappear forever, just so I wouldn't have to live with that failure any longer.'

I swallowed hard, my fingers clenching around the handle of Greta's heavy basket.

'Well,' Marina said briskly, 'I was an idiot. That's all there is to it.' She turned and gave me a dangerous flash of her eyes, like a dragon who might be resting – for now – but who could easily be provoked into shooting flame. 'There's *no one* who can do everything right all the time, Aventurine. No one! And there are some moments in all our lives that we'd take back if we could. But when I had my own little downfall ...' Her face squeezed tight. 'Well, I lost everything, that's all. My chocolate house, my position, my so-called friends ... all gone because of one night's carelessness and stupid overconfidence.'

She glared down at her hand where it rested on the rim of the fountain beside me. 'So. I know what it's like to want to hide away and lick your wounds where no one knows you. But –' she looked back up at me, her expression fierce – 'do you think I stayed that way forever, locked away feeling sorry for myself? No. I found Horst, and he was interested in setting up a new venture, too. He had his own reasons for leaving Villenne, his own problems there that he didn't mind escaping. So we thought about it, and we picked Drachenburg. Nice busy city in a rich kingdom with good trading links all around the world ... and far enough from Villenne that nobody here would know our names. Not a bad place to start over, all in all. That's what we thought, anyway.' She sighed as she looked up at me.

'I'm sorry,' I mumbled. It was the first time in my life that I'd ever spoken those words out loud, and they squeezed out of my throat like gravel as I met her eyes. My shoulders hunched in on each other as if I could fold myself out of sight. 'I know I ruined it for you.'

'What?' She stared at me. 'Have you been listening to a single word I've said?'

I stared back at her, lost.

Marina shook her head. 'I'm telling you why I ruined it, Aventurine! Why I had that moment of madness when the king and his family first arrived! I'm telling you ...' She stopped and gulped for breath as if she'd been running so hard she had run out of air. 'I'm telling you that sometimes, when you've failed before, it feels impossible to see past that failure. It can leap out at you when you least expect it. But –' she gave me a ferocious glare – 'that's no excuse not to keep trying! If we lose the Chocolate Heart, so what? We'll start again, that's all, even if we have to walk across five different kingdoms to do it. Did you really think I'd give up that easily?'

I could barely breathe. 'But ... you didn't ruin any-thing. I was the one who was left in charge. It was my job to protect the shop when the lord mayor's people came. I –'

'That's right,' Marina said, 'and whose fault was that? Who left an apprentice of less than two weeks in charge of our whole chocolate house, just when we most needed someone with experience at the helm?'

She gave an impatient huff of breath. 'The answer to

that question would be *both* me and Horst, in case you hadn't worked that out for yourself. I might make the best chocolate in Drachenburg, but I'm not the one who's best at handling diplomatic scenes. That's Horst's job, and he wasn't there that day either. No, we were both busy shouting at each other upstairs, just when we were most needed down in our shop.' Her nostrils flared. 'But I can't say it made my day any better when the best apprentice I've ever had upped and ran away just as I was taking in the mess that we'd created!'

I stopped breathing entirely. My eyes fixed on hers.

She shook her head in disgust as she looked back at me. 'For heaven's sake, girl, don't pretend to be a fool. You might have burned those tarts in all the confusion, but I tasted that hot chocolate you made.'

I coughed out my held breath. 'And?' I whispered.

She shrugged. 'Not bad,' she said judiciously. 'Especially for a first attempt.'

My chest expanded. My shoulders straightened. My lips curved into what must have been the silliest grin in the history of human existence.

I'd made my first hot chocolate, and it had been *not bad*. Marina herself had said so! And she never, ever gave an unearned compliment.

'Horst didn't even mind the tarts,' Marina told me. 'I was going to tip them all out, they were so charred, but he snagged one and ate it anyway. He said ...' She frowned. 'What was it again? Oh yes. He claimed it tasted "like they usually smell before they're cooked".'

My eyes widened. 'Like ... what?'

Something about that line felt so familiar ... *oh!* Wasn't that what I'd thought as I'd made those tarts in the first place? *Please let them taste as good once they're baked as they smell now ...*

'Nonsense really,' said Marina, 'but that's Horst for you. He's always wanted to be a poet, though you wouldn't guess it to look at him. Still, that friend of yours who wrote the handbill – she drank a good two cups of your hot chocolate that day, and she's been raving about the chocolate house ever since. Can't stand the idea of not saving it.'

'Really?' That didn't sound like cynical, sophisticated Silke.

'Mm-hmm.' She nodded, her face impossible to read. 'She put a lot of work into finding you, too.'

I frowned, trying to work that one out. 'So that I can make more hot chocolates for her?'

'Hmmph,' said Marina. 'You'll have to ask her that question yourself, if you really can't figure out the answer.' She heaved herself to her feet. 'Now, I don't know about you, but I have to get back to work. I don't have time to sit around gossiping like a nobleman.'

'Right,' I said numbly. I clutched the basket on my lap. This was it? She was leaving?

'So?' Marina said. 'What do you think?' She gave me a hard look. 'Are you going to hide away forever, just to keep yourself safe from ever failing again? Or are you ready to throw out that batch of your life that went sour, mix yourself up a new one and work to your last breath to make it the best you possibly can?' She crossed her strong arms. 'In other words, apprentice ... are you coming with me or not?'

I stared at her open-mouthed. For a moment everything hovered in the balance. And then ...

A ferocious, dragonish roar of joy erupted inside my chest as I flung out my arms, threw Greta's market basket as far as I could and chose my passion for chocolate with everything I had in me.

Vegetables and fruit and bags of grain scattered across the tiles for the pigeons to discover as I leaped to my feet, tipped back my head and let my roar escape into the market square. Maybe no one could see it any more, but I knew my tail was lashing wildly, and my wings billowed out to their full expanse as I threw my human arms into the air.

Marina's deep laughter surrounded me as I leaped and turned in dizzy circles in front of the fountain, sending pigeons scurrying and making the humans around me stare and point and whisper as if they'd never seen a happy dragon before.

'I'll take that as a yes, shall I?' Still grinning, Marina shook her head and started away, ignoring all of our shocked human onlookers. 'You'd best get all your fidgets out now, girl, before we get back. There won't be any wild whirling in my kitchen – I can tell you that right now. The last thing we need is broken crockery on our hands.'

'Don't worry.' I wheeled into place behind her, my wide, beaming smile encompassing Silke as she slipped out from the crowd to join us. 'I would never let that happen.'

I was a dragon, after all. And that meant there was nothing more important than protecting my hoard and my family ... especially when I knew exactly how close I'd come to losing them.

'Everything sorted?' Silke asked, as she fell into step beside me. 'Good. Because I have to tell you, Aventurine, I am more than ready for another of your hot chocolates. And –'

'*Aventurine?*' Greta's shriek rang in my ears as she pushed her way through the crowd to reach us. 'What in the world are you doing? Where is my basket? And who *are* these people you're talking to?' Gasping, she thudded to a halt in front of us and placed one hand over her heart. 'Oh dear.' Shaking her head sorrowfully, she turned towards Marina, her gaze sliding with open horror over Silke's coat and trousers along the way. 'I don't know what stories this wicked, ungrateful girl has told you, but this is my maid-servant, and she is not allowed to –'

'Actually,' Marina said firmly, 'she works at my chocolate house. She's been my apprentice for the last two weeks.'

'What?' Greta's mouth fell open.

'I don't remember ever letting you go, do you, Aventurine?' Marina raised her eyebrows.

I grinned back at her, relief coursing through my body like liquid gold. 'No, I left all on my own. I wasn't thrown out.'

'So you broke your apprenticeship contract? Hmm.' Silke shook her head sternly and made a *ts*king sound between her teeth. 'The town council wouldn't like that, you know! What does the law have to say about employers who lure apprentices away from their contracts?' She cocked her head innocently as she looked at Greta. 'Is it only a fine, or is it three days in prison? I just can't remember off the top of my head. Can you?'

Greta made a gargling sound in her throat. 'I – the council – what? *What?*'

'Perhaps,' Silke said sweetly, 'you might decide just to give Aventurine her first week's wages and be done with the whole matter?'

'I – but – I don't have to pay her. I was *being kind to her!*' Greta sputtered. 'And did you say ... chocolate house? *Aventurine?*'

'Forget it,' I said to Silke, and shook my head. 'Here.' I pulled Greta's unspent coins from my pocket and threw them towards her. 'You'll find your basket by the fountain. The pigeons might not have eaten all the food yet. Anything they did eat, though, you can take out from my wages.'

'*Wages?*' Greta wailed. 'But I never ... !'

'Ready to get back to work?' Marina asked me.

I pulled off my bonnet and flung it to the ground, setting my short hair free. 'Absolutely.'

'Mmm,' Silke hummed, and smiled as if she was smelling hot chocolate already.

Together the three of us walked away, leaving Greta stammering uselessly behind us.

CHAPTER 18

When I walked back into the Chocolate Heart after three days away, bright sunlight shone through the glass windows, lighting up the red and gold of the painted walls until they glowed like the heart of a flame. It felt so warm and welcoming it took me a moment to realise that every single table in the front room was empty.

Horst slammed through the swinging doors from the kitchen, his eyes wide and his smile full of teeth ... until he saw us.

'Oh.' His shoulders slumped. 'It's only you.'

Marina rolled her eyes. 'I did bring our apprentice back, in case you hadn't noticed.'

'What? Oh. Sorry.' He gave me an apologetic half-curve of his lips. 'Good to see you, Aventurine. I'm glad we didn't chase you away after all. Did Marina tell you that I liked your tarts?'

They were nice words to hear. But as his gaze swept over the empty tables, I saw his shoulders sag even further.

I felt my own mood sag along with them. 'So nobody's coming in at all any more?'

Marina's jaw tightened. 'If they all want to be frightened away by lies and gossip, I say let them. There's no reason we need to stay in Drachenburg forever. I don't mind starting over somewhere new after the rent runs out.'

Horst didn't even bother to look at her as he spoke, sounding as weary and well practised as if they'd been repeating this exact debate for the past three days. 'That would be all well and good if we *had* the money to start over. But since you know perfectly well that we don't –'

'Anyway, you can't move,' said Silke briskly. 'Just think of me! This is my city. I can't leave it. And what other chocolate house in Drachenburg would ever let me hang about and drink hot chocolates in the kitchen whenever I feel a need?'

Marina snorted. 'And on that note ...' She strode towards the kitchen. 'Come along, Aventurine. I want you to try making hot chocolate again, but under my supervision this time.'

I hurried after her, Silke by my side. But I couldn't help taking one last look, before the swinging doors closed behind us, at Horst's bowed shoulders as he surveyed the empty room.

I admired Marina more than anyone else in the whole

world. But I couldn't help but wonder whether Horst might have a better understanding of money.

I'd grown up sleeping every night upon gold and precious jewellery. I would have given anything to have even a fraction of my old bedding with me now, for the chocolate house's sake.

But that – with a sudden jolt – made me remember my new bedding. I raced to the cupboard where I'd left my scale-cloth ... and let out a gusting sigh of relief as I pulled it out. *There.*

The cloth rippled over my hands in a flood of silver and crimson, my beautiful scales overlapping and interlacing with each other in perfect harmony. The sight of them pierced my chest. I had to clench my hands around the cloth to stop myself from pressing it against my face in front of the others, or letting out any tears of sheer relief.

They noticed anyway, of course. It was useless to try to hide what I was feeling from either of those two.

'Don't worry,' said Marina, without looking up from her hand-cleaning, 'I didn't disturb it while you were gone. Nice to have one piece of bright colour left in here, even now that you've started dressing like a tree ... just like almost everyone else in this city.' She snorted as she gave a sidelong glance at Silke's own dark green outfit.

'I beg your pardon,' said Silke. 'This is my spying outfit. I needed to blend in so that I could sneak Aventurine out.'

She wandered over and ran one long brown finger

over my scale-cloth. It was a sign of how much I'd come to trust her that I didn't even snarl as she did it.

'I remember you wearing this when we first met. Funny thing.' Her eyebrows lowered as she studied it. 'I didn't pay too much attention to the pattern back then. But these almost look like –'

'No more chattering!' Marina barked, crossing her arms. 'Aventurine, I hope you're ready to work. And as for you ...' She glowered at Silke. 'If you expect to be allowed to drink what we make, then you'd better get busy yourself. If you don't have any more fancy handbills to write, then you can get started dealing with all those dirty dishes.' She nodded to the sink, which was full of crockery, pots and kettles. Apparently, the lack of customers hadn't stopped Marina from cooking up a storm.

'Will do,' Silke said cheerfully, taking off her jacket. 'But I warn you, I'll expect something seriously special as a reward.'

'You're in my kitchen, aren't you?'

'Good enough.' Silke started to whistle as she pumped up water for the sink.

I closed my eyes, breathed in the scent of roasting cocoa beans and knew without a doubt that I was home.

The sensation of sweet relief only lasted for a minute, though. Marina started rearranging the counter, setting it up for hot chocolate, while I tucked my scale-cloth back into the cupboard and cleaned my own hands. I was smiling as I began, but the sound of dishes clattering loudly against the countertop made the smile drop away from my face and the muscles in my back turn rock hard. I knew exactly what that noise meant when it came from Marina, who was more than capable of working in near silence.

For all her confident statements to Horst and to me, Marina wasn't nearly as calm as she was pretending.

Before any sly tendrils of guilt could start creeping in on me again, I quashed them hard. This wasn't my fault, no matter what I'd spent the last three days thinking ... and real dragons didn't give up on their hoards even when protecting them seemed impossible.

We'd come so close to salvation with Silke's first attempt. If only the king and his daughters had actually had a chance to drink the hot chocolate themselves ... if only the timing had been just a fraction better ...

'All right, girl,' Marina said, interrupting my thoughts. 'I want you to stand right here and make me a hot chocolate, exactly the same way you did it last time. No changes! I'm not going to say a word until you're done ... this time. I'm just going to watch. Then we'll try again, and *then* you'll need to learn about adapting your technique for different flavours and tastes.'

'I'll be happy to drink that first batch for you,' Silke called out, over the clanging sound of the pump and the gurgle of water rushing up into the sink. 'I'm telling you, Aventurine, by the time I finished my first cup of your last hot chocolate, I was *committed* to saving this place, no matter what!'

Marina rolled her eyes. 'And now that the expert on chocolate has spoken ...'

'I mean it.' Silke shrugged. 'Before I drank it, I was more than ready to move on as soon as I'd got my payment. I would've helped Aventurine find a new place to work, of course, but that was as far as it ever would've gone. By the time I'd finished that first cup of chocolate, though ...' She flashed us a grin over her shoulder.

'I see,' Marina said. 'So now we're stuck with you.' She tucked away a smile almost before I could catch it, and reached out to point me towards the charcoal brazier. 'Better get started. That one –' she tilted her head towards Silke – 'has already eaten me out of hearth and home these last few days, when she wasn't bombarding me with a dozen mad marketing ideas every half hour. It's time for you to supply her stomach, too ... if you can remember how to do it.'

That part, at least, wasn't a problem. I might have been gone for three days, but every inch of the kitchen of the Chocolate Heart was home. Working in it felt just as natural as stretching my wings once had.

As I started gathering my ingredients, though, something twitched in my memory, like a half-glimpsed moving shadow in the distance, just close enough to signal possible danger. Something that Silke had said ... and what Horst had said to Marina about the tarts ...

'Come on,' Marina said, as my fingers stilled above the mountain of crushed sugar. 'Don't freeze up on me now, girl. If you can make hot chocolate for the king himself without any real training, you can make it for me, too. Just put yourself back into that moment when you thought it all out the first time.'

I frowned.

I hadn't thought it out the first time actually. I'd used what I'd learned from memorising Marina's every action, and then I'd flown the rest of the way on sheer instinct. No: on desperation. I'd been so desperate to convince the royal family that this chocolate house should be saved, I would have done anything to convince them with my chocolate. Just like ...

Something shivered in the back of my mind. Something like a piece of knowledge that I did not want to have.

Or a memory I didn't want to remember.

Someone else shivering with fear as he made my hot chocolate ... murmuring over it as I watched ... weaving his own desperation into my bones, until I lost all control, lost everything that mattered, even ...

No. I forced down the remembered panic, steeling my spine into rigidity with the reminder: there were no food mages with me in this kitchen. I'd never have to deal with one again. They were so rare that just the hint of one had been enough to fill our front room with customers. Even the king himself had never met one.

I never wanted to meet another one in my life.

'Easy,' Marina murmured. 'Don't think so much. Just decide what you want to do, and do it.'

Do it.

My hands started moving.

I had to erase that memory of helplessness and fear. I had to make something new to replace it before it could rise up and break my spirit again, the way I'd felt broken and hollow over the past few days. I had to fill myself with the unshakeable certainty of something true. Something undeniable. Something powerful.

Me.

So I yanked my heart and my mind wide open at last and I let all the other memories sweep in upon me in a blaze of fire, all those memories that I'd been trying so hard to hold back for the past two weeks. Memories of scales and claws and the effortless certainty of power; essential parts of myself that had hurt so much to lose, I'd locked them away where they could only haunt my dreams. They were memories of the dragon I had been before … *no!* The dragon I still was, underneath it all.

I'm the fiercest thing in this city.

I *am.*

Greta had been wrong about me after all, so wrong. But I'd been wrong to let myself believe her, too – wrong to lower my head and let myself be chained by soft, cruel, laughing words and a poisonous pity that had tasted more bitter than any ingredient in Marina's kitchen ever could.

I wasn't that helpless creature that Greta had made of me over the past few days. But she had managed it only because secretly, in my heart, I'd feared that might be who I had become, ever since my first moment of transformation. I'd looked at my puny human body and felt despair. I'd believed, in my secret heart, that I was every bit as much a failure as my own family had expected me to be.

No more.

I was an apprentice chocolatier at the best chocolate house in Drachenburg.

I was a dragon and I was a human girl, at one and the same time.

I was better than I'd ever been before.

I was *me*.

I stirred in the last of the ingredients and let all of that certainty flood into my firm, steady strokes. I *can be whatever I want to be, forever*.

And with that certainty came peace.

When the kettle was ready, I took my time with the wooden molinet, frothing the chocolate into creamy perfection. I poured it into a porcelain cup under Marina's watchful eye.

Then I started to hand it to Silke, who'd finished washing dishes and was waiting – but to my surprise she shook her head and stepped back.

'I'll have the second cup,' she said. 'You never managed to drink any of your own chocolate last time. It's only fair to let you drink first, this time round.'

I looked at Marina. She nodded, her lips quirking.

'How else do you plan to improve?' she asked me. 'You've got to taste all of your own attempts, you know, to find out exactly what you can do.'

I *can do this*.

And maybe – if I'd done it well enough – it would give me the courage to do something else, too: finally tell my new family the whole truth of who I was, beneath my skin.

I picked up the porcelain cup in my hands and felt its

heat flood up my arms and through my small – but *not* puny – human body. Half closing my eyes, I lifted the cup towards my mouth.

The bell over the front door of the shop jingled loudly before I could take a single sip.

My eyes flew open as I lowered the cup. *Customers?* I could tell from Marina's suddenly frozen expression that she was thinking the same thing.

Silke started for the peephole. Before she could even touch the plate that covered it, the kitchen doors flew open.

A tall, skinny boy with dark brown skin, glasses and wide, panicked eyes stood panting in the doorway. Horst hurried up behind him, mouth open as if to demand answers, but the boy spoke first.

'Silke!' He grabbed the doorway as if to hold himself up. 'I can't believe I've finally found you. I've been hunting everywhere!'

Aha. I recognised him now – Silke's brother.

Silke frowned back at him. 'Oh, honestly, Dieter. What's the matter now? I told you I wouldn't be back to help at the stall until –'

He gave an impatient swipe of his free hand. 'That doesn't matter,' he said. 'Not any more. I needed to tell you ... warn all of you ...' His eyes, full of dread behind his narrow spectacles, turned to Marina and me as well, as if the panic inside him was too large to hold alone.

'You can see them yourself by now, if you step outside.' Dieter pointed one shaking finger back towards the big

182

glass windows of the front room. 'The rumours started coming in half an hour ago that they'd been spotted. I didn't believe it at first. No one really did. But they're moving so fast there's no mistaking them ... and no escaping.' He swallowed visibly. 'No one's going to get away in time.'

'From what?' Horst grabbed Dieter's shoulder and shook him. 'What are you talking about, boy?'

But somehow I already knew.

'Dragons,' Dieter whispered. 'A whole pack of them, from the mountains. They're flying straight towards Drachenburg.'

CHAPTER 19

I barely caught my cup as it slipped through my hands, and my chest pierced with longing so bright that it hurt. *They'd come for me!*

But ...

No, I told myself firmly, and wrapped my fingers securely around the porcelain cup, letting the heat of it anchor me. *Don't be stupid.*

The last time I had tried to go home, I'd had a fireball flung at me to warn me well away. So they definitely hadn't come for me, no matter what my stupid, treacherous heart might have hoped for one brief moment.

But even if I wasn't a real part of my first family any more, I still knew their rules. They always avoided humans whenever possible, even when those humans were alone. If they were really on their way to a crowded human city now, after the kind of restless, reckless behaviour that the humans had been gossiping about for at least a week ... then something had gone very wrong indeed.

And no matter what those stupid battle mages might think, everyone in this city was in danger.

Breathing hard, I set my cup down safely on the closest counter, next to the presentation pot with the rest of the hot chocolate I had cooked.

Around me, a jumble of voices filled the kitchen.

'Dragons?'

'But – !'

'Why – ?'

'We have to hide!' Dieter yanked free of Horst's grip. 'We can't stand around talking!'

Marina's golden skin looked almost grey, but she stood her ground. 'And where exactly do you think we should go, young man? If a pack of dragons is really intent on attacking this city, they'll burn every building to the ground. There's nowhere that we can hide.'

'By the river,' Dieter said urgently. 'It's the only safe way. I know we'll be out in the open there, but at least if we're near water we might have a chance to –'

'But *why* are dragons attacking us?' Silke interrupted him. 'It makes no sense! I know there were always scare stories about travellers sighting dragons out by the mountains, but they've never come anywhere near a real city before. Why – ?'

'Who cares?' Dieter demanded. He reached out to grab her arm.

Silke danced back. 'I'm still thinking!' Her eyes narrowed. 'Look, if *we* already know about the dragons, the king must, too. And you know there's been that whole movement among the merchants lately, pushing for him to send soldiers and battle mages into the mountains and clear out any dragon nests for good. I'll bet you anything he's already ordered the army out by now, not to mention every battle mage he's got. Any dragons on their way will be slaughtered before they can blow a single flame near the city.'

'No!' I lurched forward, my voice a ravaged croak. 'A battalion won't be enough. Battle mages won't be enough. And they *cannot* attack before they even know what the dragons want. If they do, it'll be a disaster!'

Dieter looked sick. 'Then –'

Silke cut him off, her sharp gaze fixed on me. 'What do you know about dragons, Aventurine?'

I looked into her eyes, and I took a deep breath. 'Do you remember all those questions you asked me about where I came from, and why I was keeping it such a secret? Well, I don't have the time to explain it all now ... but if we really are friends, then I need you to believe me. There *will* be a slaughter if the king sends out his army. But it won't be the dragons who are killed.' I looked at Marina. 'You're right. They'll burn every street of the city down in retribution if the army attacks them.'

I could almost hear Grandfather's voice in my head,

186

planning strategy. *If these humans aren't punished in a way that sends fear into the hearts of everyone else who might ever think to plan such carnage ...*

I couldn't let it happen. Not in the city that had become my territory.

The last time I'd tried to call out to Grandfather, he'd sent a fireball arcing towards me. But any dragon worth her scales would brave far worse to protect her hoard and the creatures who had become her family. And this room was full of those.

I wouldn't let any of them be hurt.

'We need to stop this,' I told Silke.

Horst gave a disbelieving crack of laughter. 'How exactly do you plan to do that? If you'd ever seen a real dragon ...'

'That's not who I need to see first.' My gaze was firmly fixed on Silke. 'You know every inch of this city. Can you find a way to take me to the king or the crown princess? I need to talk to one of them. *Now.*'

Silke stared at me. Then she began to laugh as she slowly shook her head back and forth. 'Oh, Aventurine,' she said, 'I always knew you were a little different from the rest of us. But until now I never knew you were completely insane.'

'Fine.' I left my untouched hot chocolate on the counter behind me as I started across the room. 'I'll find a way myself then.' *Somehow.* 'But –'

'Oh no you won't.' Silke tucked her hand in my arm as she fell into step beside me. 'Trust me, I wouldn't miss this for the world. And besides –' she looked me pityingly up and down – 'let's face it: you may be a fantastic apprentice chocolatier, but you're no more dressed for a royal visit now than you were when you first arrived in this city. And when it comes to talking your way past royal guards while you're dressed like a housemaid ... ? You could really use me on your side.'

Well, *that* was why I'd asked her in the first place. But I felt a ball of unfamiliar warmth form, like a quiet, steady flame in my chest, as I looked into her face and saw the smile lurking there.

And speaking of how I was dressed ...

I pulled free and hurried to the cupboard where my scale-cloth was kept. It might not help me with the king, but if Silke ever managed to get me past all the battle-hungry humans who were involved in this mess, I'd be talking to my family soon. This time I'd have to find a way to make them listen.

I only had one good-luck talisman in my possession – and it was exactly what I needed to remind myself of who I really was, both human skin *and* scales included.

Marina was right. It was time to stop hiding and flash some colour.

I tucked the silver-and-crimson scale-cloth under my arm and strode back towards Silke, ready to risk dragonfire.

'This is ridiculous!' Dieter darted in front of us before we could even reach the swinging doors. 'Silke, I know you've never had an ounce of common sense, but I'm telling you: you can't just go trotting off across the city *when there are dragons flying towards it!*'

Silke raised one eyebrow. 'If there are dragons flying towards us,' she said, 'I'd rather spend my last minutes having a wild adventure instead of cowering in fear.'

He glowered down at her, crossing his arms. 'You are *only thirteen years old!*' he told her. 'And if Mother and Father were here, they'd tell you how stupid and irresponsible you were being!'

'No,' said Marina abruptly. 'Actually, she's right. Horst?' She looked at him. 'I don't know about you, but if this is the last hour of my life, I want to spend it doing what's most important. Do you remember that question you keep on asking me?'

Horst stared at her. Then he straightened away from the wall with a wild jerk. 'Now?' he said. '*Now's* when you finally agree to marry me?'

Marina snorted. 'Are you mad? Where would we find a judge at this time of day, without any notice?' She gestured at the stove. 'No, I was talking about the chocolate.'

'Of course you were.' Horst rolled his eyes, but his shoulders relaxed. A half-smile broke across his face. 'So you're finally willing to try my experiment? You'll actually make a chocolate custard to my recipe instead of yours?'

'Why not?' Marina smiled back at him as she picked up a wooden spoon. 'It'll taste horrific, of course, and it's an abomination of my kitchen ... but if we're all about to be burned up anyway, I might as well make you happy, this once.' She pointed the spoon at him threateningly. 'I'm warning you, though: if we survive, you'll have to eat every bit of this disaster, even if that means licking the whole pot clean. And I don't want any complaints!'

Horst's smile thinned as he gave a gentle shake of his head. 'Unlike the rest of you,' he said quietly, 'I've actually seen a dragon. It was a long time ago, and from a long way away ... but no. I don't think survival will be a possibility for us today.' He sighed and pushed the kitchen doors open. 'I'll get a table and chairs from the front room. Dieter? Do you want to stay and enjoy the new recipe?'

Dieter gaped at all of us, shaking his head. 'Everyone in this kitchen is mad, except for me.'

'Well, then,' Silke said, her smile razor-sharp, 'it's no wonder I like it here so much. Step aside, big brother.'

As the two of them locked gazes, I looked back at Marina, bracing myself. 'I really do have to go.'

'I understand.' She gave me a firm nod. 'Go. See if you can bash any sense into the king's thick head. But then come back ... because I'm not losing my apprentice again.'

I'd genuinely thought, by then, that I must have walked through almost all the streets of Drachenburg. I was wrong.

Silke led me down narrow twisting back alleys I'd never seen before, and under bridges where frightened people huddled together in clumps, many of them holding massive sacks that seemed to be filled with their most precious possessions.

Every time I looked into the sky and saw those still-tiny

but unmistakable winged figures in the far distance, I lost my breath. My chest felt close to bursting with so many emotions mixed together that I couldn't even tell which one of them was the strongest.

None of the humans around me seemed to have that problem, though. They were simply terrified.

I thought about telling them that there was no need to hide under bridges. For one thing, the dragons were still too far away to shoot flames at them. For another, the bridges wouldn't do them any good once the dragons finally did arrive. It would have made much more sense for all of these cowering people to stay outside, enjoying their city while they still could and savouring what might be their very last minutes.

But it was always hard to tell how humans would react to good advice, and I had enough to worry about, protecting this whole city.

'This isn't the way to the palace, is it?' I asked Silke, as she led me at a quick trot through the chaos of a busy second-district street clogged by carriages. Half the city – or at least anyone with enough money to own a vehicle – seemed to be trying to escape. The traffic had come to a standstill, with each horse's nose nearly bumping the back of the next carriage. Drivers shouted at each other from every direction, and finely dressed men and women leaned out of the carriage windows to add their own screeching to the chaos, holding massive cases on their laps and looking just as panicked as the horses.

'The palace? Why would we want to go there?' Silke

dodged around a snorting carriage-horse as she darted ahead of me towards the pavement. The horse reared, letting out a whinny of rage, and the driver screamed an insult that I didn't understand. Silke waved a dismissive hand at the driver as I stopped walking to stare down the horse.

'You couldn't have moved forward anyway!' Silke called back to the human. 'No one's going anywhere in this crush. So there's no reason to be rude!'

Then she grabbed my hand and pulled me away from my staring match to a gap between the two shops ahead of us. It led to a bare, unpainted passageway barely wide enough for the two of us to squeeze through, with a gutter running down it and sending a terrible stench into the air.

'No one important will be at the palace,' Silke told me as we hurried down the stinking passageway, skipping carefully around the channel of dirty water at its centre. 'The king and the crown princess would never stay there in a crisis. They'll be at the town hall, along with the lord mayor and the king's privy council – they're like the town council, but they look after the whole country. Oh, and the head of the army should be there, too, by now. They all have to be *seen* to be working together, for politics' sake, even if the king is the only one who can make a final decision when it comes to war.'

Humans. Their rules would never make sense to me.

But at least it looked as if I would finally have a chance to meet the man who'd been trying so hard to destroy the Chocolate Heart from the time I'd first arrived in Drachenburg. My teeth bared in a menacing smile at the thought of the lord mayor, and my short human nails bit into my palms like claws.

'No attacking anybody!' Silke said, without even looking back at me. 'Remember, let me do the talking.'

'Hmmph.'

I didn't mind letting her do the *talking*, at least when it came to the humans in our way. But I wasn't making any promises about the attacking.

No *one* threatened my hoard without retribution.

'Well' – Silke blew out her breath as she led me out the other end of the passageway, on to the edge of a wide, open square – 'it looks like everyone's here already.'

A massive grey stone building rose up at the far end of the square, covered with carved gargoyles that crawled along its rows and rows of arching windows. The whole effect was probably supposed to look impressive, but to me it looked as bumpy and over-decorated as the kind of fancy cake that Marina always sneered at. She said that *real* cooks cared more about taste than about appearance.

Still, even I had to admit that it was big. High, pointed stone towers shot up from every corner. The central tower stood highest of all, with a huge clock facing out from the top of it. I'd seen that clock tower a hundred times before, from all around Drachenburg … and as my gaze fixed on it now, a real plan finally formed in my head, as clear and right as any of Marina's recipes.

Of course, even the best recipes didn't work when the wrong cook tried them. But …

From the top of that tower, a person would be able to

see everything. She would be the first thing that a dragon would see, too.

'It's perfect,' I told Silke, and pointed to the clock tower high above us. 'All I have to do is get up there!'

'Oh?' Silke sighed. 'Well, good luck with that.' She pushed down on my arm until it was pointing straight ahead at the city square in front of the building, packed with men in red-and-black uniforms, carrying weapons that glinted in the sunlight. 'Because you'll have to get past all of *them* first.'

CHAPTER 20

I scowled at the lines of stiff-backed men in uniform. There must have been at least a hundred of them, all heavily armed, and every one of them was in my way. 'What are they doing here?'

'Protecting the royal family and the privy council, most likely.' Silke gnawed on her lower lip, frowning. 'I knew they'd have an honour guard, but I didn't think there'd be this many soldiers here. They must be planning to hole up in the town hall if there's a final siege. I guess this'll be the last line of defence for the city, while the royals and the lord mayor stay safe inside those stone walls.'

'Safe?' I snorted, copying Marina's favourite sound of disdain. 'Do they actually think dragons can't set stone on fire?'

The whites of Silke's eyes suddenly looked enormous. 'They *can*?'

I shrugged. 'We're talking about dragonfire, not kitchen flame.'

'But – no, never mind.' Silke squared her shoulders. 'Later you'll have to explain how you know all this. But for now ...' She gave me a firm look. 'No clenching your fists. No meeting anyone's eyes. Remember: you're a lowly housemaid, and you work for someone just like that awful Greta woman. You know what that's like. Head down ... and *go*!'

She grabbed my arm and started forward, dragging me behind her.

She barely made it five steps before she was hailed. 'You there!' A soldier who didn't look any older than Dieter marched forward to bar our way, drawing his sword. 'What are you doing this close to the town hall?'

'What do you think?' Silke replied. I had my eyes firmly fixed on the ground, following orders, but even I could hear the eye-roll in her voice. She let out a heavy sigh, too, as she yanked me around to stand in front of her.

Gritting my teeth, I let her do it.

'I've found the crown princess's maid at last,' Silke said. 'She'd made it halfway across the city by the time I caught up with her, trying to run away. Stupid girl!'

'Oh. Um.' The young soldier's voice nearly cracked, but I could feel him eyeing me up and down, and every inch of my skin prickled with aggression in response. I wanted to lift my eyes and bare my teeth and glare him down until he went skittering back and ...

No! I whispered to myself. *Not a dragon. Not right now.*

The moment seemed to last forever, but he finally let out a snort and shook his head. 'Got scared and ran, did she? Abandoned her post?' His voice came out bigger this time, as if he'd somehow put on an extra few inches of muscle just by looking at someone even more frightened than him. Worse yet, his tone sweetened, adding a sickly shade of condescension as he reached forward and tapped his finger under my chin. 'You don't need to worry, sweetheart. We'll take care of any dragons that threaten this city.'

My family would eat you in a heartbeat, I snarled silently. But I kept my mouth clamped shut with all my might, and I didn't even try to bite his finger off as he pulled it back from under my chin.

'Oh, you know what ignorant country folk are like,' Silke told him. 'But you're from Drachenburg originally, aren't you? I can tell just by looking at you.'

The soldier's shoulders straightened and his chin lifted an extra notch. 'I am!'

'I knew it,' Silke said. 'It's just so obvious that you know what *you're* doing.' She leaned closer, confidingly, without letting go of my arm. 'We'd better get this idiot back to the crown princess, though, as soon as possible. Of all the times to neglect her duties to the royal family ...'

'Of course!' The soldier wheeled around. 'Just wait here.'

He marched away, moving every bit as stiffly as the little clockwork men I'd watched in that toyshop window, during my afternoon off. The idea of him fighting my family ...

I said, through my teeth, 'If he touches my chin again, I'll eat him.'

'Don't worry about him,' Silke said. 'Worry about the next round.'

Sure enough, when he came back a moment later he was accompanied by an older man with dull grey hair and two bright stripes on the shoulder of his uniform. 'The crown princess's maidservant, eh?' The new soldier looked me up and down with narrowed eyes, and I didn't need Silke's warning arm-squeeze to keep my gaze lowered and my mouth shut. 'I didn't hear anything about this,' he rumbled in a cave-deep voice.

'I'm not surprised,' Silke said. 'It happened just on the way out of the palace.' She shrugged. 'We realised she'd gone missing before anyone had even stepped into the first carriage, so I promised the crown princess I'd hunt her down and bring her back. She's new to service, you know, and she panicked at the thought of dragons, but she knows her duty now. She won't abandon her mistress again.'

'Hmmph.' The man looked from one to the other of us. 'And why aren't either of you girls wearing palace uniform, if this little story is true?'

I looked at Silke out of the corner of my eyes.

She smiled straight at him. 'She wasn't going to keep her uniform on when she ran away, now, was she? She's not *that* much of an idiot. And the princess prefers me to stay out of uniform, always, to be her eyes and ears in the city.'

Then she cocked her head as she studied him just as frankly as he had studied me. 'Right now, though, major, I have to ask *you* a question: exactly who do you think we really are, if you find the truth so doubtful? Do you imagine that we're dragons in disguise?' She snorted, even as my hand tightened on my scale-cloth. 'I don't know what *you're* afraid of, but I know what frightens me … and that's the crown princess, if she finds out we've been kept chin-wagging out here when I was ordered to bring back her new maid as soon as possible. So –' she took a step forward, dropping my arm, and met his eyes full-on – 'if you have any more questions,' she said sweetly, 'why don't you put them to the crown princess yourself?'

I'd always known that Silke had a touch of dragon to her. But as I watched her stare down the big man, I could almost see the scales that she deserved glinting in the air around her.

'*There's such a thing as friendship,*' she had told me in the market square.

For the first time, I truly understood what she'd meant. Because I knew then that I would fight on her side forever.

The man's jaw worked as he glared back at her. His hand fell to the handle of his sword.

But then he stepped backwards and lowered his head. 'Very well.' His voice came out as a low, angry growl. 'Lieutenant –' he jerked his head at the younger soldier – 'don't leave them on their own in the royal apartments. I want you to escort them to the crown princess *personally* and see exactly what she says. Then report back to me.'

Silke nodded with cool authority. 'Thank you, Major. That will do.' She turned back to me but didn't grab my arm this time. 'Come along, *Eva*.'

Oh, I would absolutely pay her back for calling me that!

But not now. Right now I followed her and the young lieutenant past row after row of armed soldiers across the square, then through the big, iron-braced oak doors of the town hall. As the doors fell closed behind us with an ominous *thunk*, I didn't even feel tempted to let out a single roar of triumph.

Yes, Silke had taken care of her part of the bargain. Now, though, it was my turn. And if I was worried about how I could handle my own family ... I had *no idea* how to make the royals see sense. Especially when they'd ignored everything I'd tried to tell them last time, in the Chocolate Heart.

Human society was so complicated. Why couldn't I just roar at people to *make* them do what was necessary?

But then, from the sounds of distant shouting that echoed down the wide corridors of the town hall, it sounded as if some humans were already trying that method.

There were even more soldiers lining the wide white-and-silver corridors inside, standing as still as stone between elaborate marble statues and tall windows. They stood stiffly in place with no expressions on their faces, no matter how heated the yelling in the distance became or how close to them we walked. Only their gazes flickered back and forth beneath their iron helmets, following us as we passed, to mark them out from the cold, sightless statues at their sides.

I would have snorted in disgust at the view around me if I hadn't been in disguise. This was the seat of all power in Drachenburg? This was the central hoard of the king's town and privy councils, their greatest chance to awe the world? Really, marble was only another word for 'dirty white stone'. I didn't see a single gold plate or sparkling diamond anywhere. Even when I tipped my head back for a quick glance at the ceiling, the looping curlicues carved there were painted white-on-white and made of simple plaster. No dragon would take this place seriously for an instant.

The thought of this city trying to protect itself against my family would have been laughable if it wasn't so horrify-ing. This was *my* territory now, for better or for worse. But I wouldn't even be allowed to defend it unless I could get past all the noisy humans in my way.

The shouting grew louder and louder with every step I took. Even if the din hadn't alerted me, I would have known exactly which door we were heading towards, because four tall soldiers stood guard outside it. They stepped aside at a word from our lieutenant, who opened the door to reveal a scene of total chaos.

The room inside was as big as a cavern, with swags of deep purple velvet hanging from the high walls, and people crowding the space on all sides. A long wooden table filled the centre of the room, with the king sitting at one end in a chair like a throne, the crown princess sitting in a smaller chair beside him and a big, scowling man with a floppy red velvet hat sitting in a medium-sized chair at the other end of the table. Half of the other chairs were filled, but the rest had been abandoned as their owners paced around the table, yelling and waving their arms.

And they weren't the only people there. Even more soldiers lined the walls by the heavy swags of purple velvet, while women and men in fancy clothing sat in rows and rows of padded chairs, watching the show in front of them and whispering to each other behind decorative fans. Servants moved back and forth between all the different groups, seeing to their masters' needs.

How did these people ever get anything done? The noise was so intense it took me a moment to even pick out any of the individual voices, as our lieutenant led us carefully through the crowd towards the table and the crown princess.

'This is why we should have sent the army and the mages into the mountains years ago! If anyone had ever listened to me ...' *That* came from a man in a dark green suit, banging on the table.

The man behind him shook his head violently. 'We should be digging tunnels underground to escape into the forest! If we set the army to digging now ...'

A tall, bony man in a black robe snarled, 'Maybe if we had been given enough funds for our research, without the merchants always haggling over prices and trying to keep all the taxes for themselves ...'

The woman next to him let out a muffled shriek of outrage. 'We merchants are the only reason this city has prospered! If you black-robed nincompoops were ever left in charge –'

Another woman, in a long black robe, lunged up from the table and shouted, 'What did you just call us, shopkeeper?'

Stones and bones. We didn't have time for any of this!

When I'd tried to talk sensibly to the royals before, they hadn't listened to a word I'd said. I could already tell that this group wasn't interested in calm reason either.

So it was time to stop acting like a servant and be a dragon, after all.

'Enough!' I roared, only two feet behind the king.

Everyone in the room jerked around to stare at me. Even the king peered around the back of his massive chair with wide, startled blue eyes.

I knew exactly what they all saw when they looked at me, with my young face, short hair and dull brown dress. I knew that their shock would only hold them silent for a moment, before their outrage and disbelief would take over.

So I used the single moment that I had, crossed my arms and gave the king a look as steady and grim as any I had ever seen from Marina.

'None of you can stop those dragons,' I told him. 'But I can.'

CHAPTER 21

That was it. The silence broke, as all around the table a dozen men and women erupted at once.

This time, though, the king's hand slashed through the air to cut them all off. 'Who *are* you?' he demanded. 'Come here, child. Explain yourself!'

I stepped forward until I stood between him and the crown princess, arms still crossed before me. As I moved, another gasp swept across the room, this one of obvious horror. Panicky whispers started up all through the group of nobles watching us from the chairs. The king's bushy blond eyebrows lowered into a scowl, and the crown princess's dark eyebrows rose high on her light brown forehead.

What had I done wrong now? I'd just been following orders.

Then I felt a hard nudge in my back, and I twisted around to see Silke glaring at me. 'Bow!' she hissed.

Oh. I uncrossed my arms and bent my whole body forward, the way I'd seen some humans do before. I nearly banged my head on the corner of the table, and a wave of tittering laughter started up from the rows of onlookers behind me, but by the time I straightened, the king's scowl had dimmed. I was vaguely aware of more people, probably servants, hurrying around the table towards the other end, but I ignored them, focusing on the two royals.

'You can't attack the dragons,' I told the king. 'They'll burn the city to the ground in retaliation if you do that. Wait and find out what they want first. They won't have come here without a reason.'

'A reason?' A woman halfway down the table let out a crack of laughter. 'They're primitive beasts, girl! Their only *reason* is they're hungry.'

The man beside her nodded. 'They're not like us,' he told me. 'They don't have the brains to want anything apart from blood and gold!'

I shook my head in disbelief. 'Don't you people know anything about dragons?'

The king's eyes narrowed as he studied me. 'I know,' he said, 'that they're the greatest danger ever to threaten this city. And you expect us to listen to an unknown young girl and not even *try* to protect ourselves from their attack?'

'You can't protect yourselves from them anyway,' I said impatiently, 'so –'

'Wait!' The man with the massive floppy hat who sat at the other end of the table leaned forward and pointed one beefy finger at me. 'Your Majesty, you are being deceived. My assistant knows this girl. She's a mere shop apprentice, *and* a known troublemaker. We need to have her thrown out, now, before she wastes another minute of this council's precious time!'

Behind his chair, a familiar face smirked straight at me. It was the lord mayor's woman ... and now I knew exactly who that man was, too. My muscles tensed.

'No, Aventurine!' Silke grabbed my shoulder. 'Not now!'

Our lieutenant started forward, wide-eyed and already reaching out as if to yank me away from the royals. Before he could, though, the crown princess raised one hand, and silence fell.

'I thought I recognised you,' she said. Despite myself, I was impressed by the power of her voice; it never rose anywhere near a shout, but her words still carried through the room with calm authority. 'Aventurine, wasn't it? From the Chocolate Heart?'

The king winced. 'Not that chocolate house they had to shut down for its dirty kitchen?'

'It was not dirty!' I snapped. 'It passed that inspection and got a certificate to prove it, too. The only reason they even bothered –'

'Ahem.' The crown princess cleared her throat. 'Be that as it may, why exactly would a young apprentice chocolatier know how to stop a ravening pack of dragons?'

Well, this was it. I looked her in the eye and said, 'Because I used to be one of them.'

Silke's hand suddenly clenched around my shoulder, even as the room exploded into noise.

There were shouts of laughter, there were howls of disbelief and there were several snorts of disdain, but through it all, I heard Silke's whisper vibrate in my ear: '*So that's it!*'

An instant later, she was darting in front of me, sweeping an elaborate bow to the royals. 'What she meant to say, Your Majesties ...'

The crown princess raised her eyebrows. 'Yes?'

Silke smiled brightly as she straightened. 'Aventurine is from the mountains. She lived in the middle of nowhere, in an eccentric family, so she had the chance to speak with these dragons herself and get to know them. So –'

'*Spy!*' bellowed the lord mayor, and started to his feet, slamming one big hand noisily against the table. 'Is *she* the reason they're coming here now? Did she feed them information about our city?'

The crown princess's eyes closed for a brief moment of what looked like extreme weariness as the yelling around the table started up again, worse than ever. Even more men and women jumped up from their seats. Others started banging their fists on the table, adding to the din. The king scowled and covered his mouth with one hand, studying me with narrowed pale blue eyes.

I had a nasty feeling that even roaring wouldn't work on these humans any more.

The crown princess didn't lift her own hand for

silence this time. She only leaned forward, speaking to me alone while the other council members filled the rest of the room with noise. 'What exactly would *you* do to stop the dragons from coming here?' she asked.

'There's no way to stop them coming now that they're already on their way,' I told her. 'You can't hurt any of them with bullets or spells; their scales are too hard for that. The only thing we can do is wait and let them come.'

'And then?' the king demanded. He was leaning forward to listen, now, too.

I shrugged. 'I'll talk to them,' I told him. 'If I can get up to the top of the clock tower, I can make myself the first thing that they see. Then I'll make them see sense.'

'Make them see – ?!' The king let out a snort so powerful it ruffled against my face. 'Oh, wonderful,' he growled. 'Our capital city's whole plan for defence: sending one young girl, who can't be more than twelve years old, to *talk things over* with a pack of fire-breathing monsters! Because everyone knows how *reasonable* dragons can be!'

A growl of my own came rumbling up my throat, vibrating through my body as I glared at him. 'You don't know anything about dragons! They'll be coming here for a real reason, not just to destroy the city. They won't do that unless you make them angry by attacking them unprovoked. *Someone's* got to talk to them, and I'm the only one who knows how to persuade them into anything.'

'I'm sorry.' The crown princess sighed, leaning back in her chair. 'You must see how impossible that is. The idea of listening to a child and allowing those monsters to fly over

208

Drachenburg undisputed – simply sitting back and waiting for them to attack, without even trying to defend our own citizens from their flame ...'

An unexpected voice spoke behind me. 'We cannot stop them from flying over the city, Your Highness.' It was the tall bony mage who'd argued with the merchants earlier. His arms were crossed and he looked down at me consideringly, with light green eyes that looked almost reptilian themselves. 'I recommend that we follow this child's suggestion.'

'You must be joking!' The king stared at him. 'You want us to put all of our protection in the hands of one unknown girl?'

'No,' said the mage. 'I want to use the girl to draw the dragons to their doom. *That* is my suggestion.'

As the four of us stared at him in shock, the mage raised one bony shoulder in a shrug. 'Well? The mages of Drachenburg have never been granted the funding we needed for serious research on penetrating dragon hide from a distance. If we try to attack while they're flying high above the city, we'll have no more luck than your soldiers with their pathetic rifle shots that bounce off dragon scales without effect. However –' his thin lips curved into a small, smug smile – 'we have recently come up with some extraordinary new attack strategies that will, I believe, work well at close range, even against the power of fully hardened, adult dragon scales. If we can use this girl as bait to draw the dragons down to the level of the clock tower, then mount a surprise attack from the floor just below while the beasts are off guard, thinking it to be a truce ...'

'That's *disgusting!*' I spat. 'And cowardly, and deceitful, and –'

He didn't even raise his voice as he spoke over me. 'That is my recommendation, as the most experienced battle mage in Drachenburg. In my considered opinion, that is the only way that we can win this battle and protect our innocent civilians. Therefore, Your Majesty ... ?' He raised one eyebrow.

The king nodded heavily. 'Yes. Let's do it. We'll have to put the motion to the council for form's sake, but I'll over-rule the others if necessary. If you start organising your mages into position now –'

'No!' I shouted. If I'd had my wings, they would have been flaring around me, higher than ever before. 'I won't trick and deceive them, not even to save this city! I told you, I can talk them into leaving peacefully. There's no reason for you to attack them – especially in such a shameful way! How can you even consider treating anyone like that?'

The king raised his upper lip in a sneer. 'Remember, we are talking about dragons, not humans, girl. There's a difference.'

'Not that much,' I told him. 'Not as much as I used to think.'

He sat forward, turning away from me. 'Young lady, we're wasting time.' He reached for his feather pen and inkwell. 'Now, you can do as you're ordered, or you can be thrown into the holding cells downstairs to stop you from creating any trouble, while someone else draws your dragons down instead. So ...'

'No one else will be able to do it,' Silke said abruptly. 'No one except for Aventurine.'

The king's head jerked around. 'And why is that, exactly?'

Silke answered before I could. 'Because she's the only one who knows the secret signal – the *peace* signal for the dragons.'

The *what*? My mouth fell open. Of all the ridiculous, unbelievable suggestions ...

But Silke was already continuing: 'How do you think she and her family survived with the dragons all those years, without a special coded signal to mark them out as dragon-friends?'

The king scowled.

The mage's eyes narrowed.

Silke nudged me. *Oh.* My turn.

'I won't tell anyone else the signal,' I snarled, lifting my chin. 'It's my family secret.'

My family would have sent smokeballs careening all around this room with their laughter at the very idea of that stupid signal. But I saw barely repressed rage on the king's reddening face, and I knew he'd been convinced.

He pointed one finger at me, opening his mouth as if to roar, but the crown princess smiled and spoke first.

'Very well,' she said smoothly. 'I propose a compromise solution. Lord Krakauer –' she nodded to the mage – 'if you would be so good as to gather your mages in place, hidden just below the clock tower, we would very much appreciate it. However –' she gave me a cool, assessing look – 'we will not order any attacks until Aventurine has attempted to negotiate the dragons' peaceful departure. Aventurine, do you agree?'

Uh-oh.

I narrowed my eyes at her, desperately trying to read the truth behind her serene, innocent expression. I knew this feeling, and I didn't like it. My sister Citrine was just this calm, pleasant and confident whenever she was using her gift with words to trick me or Jasper into doing something we would absolutely hate.

The crown princess was definitely hiding something ... but there was no time to quibble. I let out my held breath in an explosive sigh. 'All ri–' I began.

Silke cut me off before I could finish. 'Your Highness,' she said, in a tone like ice, 'don't *you* mean to promise, instead, that you won't order any attacks until Aventurine has *failed* to negotiate the dragons' peaceful departure?'

Oh. Oh! That was why it had felt so wrong!

Irritation flashed across the crown princess's face.

She was just like Citrine, after all.

'You were trying to trick me,' I breathed. 'You were going to order the attack as soon as I first started trying to negotiate with them, weren't you?'

And in that case ... Oh. I glared at her. 'How did you think I was going to survive that attack, when the mages went after the dragons right beside me?'

The crown princess gave me a smile that I didn't

believe in for a second. 'Forgive me,' she said sweetly, 'but what else could we do? After all, none of the rest of us knows your special peace signal. If you negotiate with the dragons alone on that clock tower, how will we know whether or not your negotiations are working? Really, we have no choice but to assume the worst, so ...'

I crossed my arms. Thinking of Citrine had given me the perfect answer.

'Fine,' I said. 'Then I won't be alone with them. I'll have one other person with me up there, who can run back down and tell you if it all goes wrong. But it'll be someone that I trust. Someone that I choose. And someone who's my own age, no older, so the dragons won't feel threatened when they see that I'm not alone.'

'You mean your friend here?' The crown princess laughed as she looked at Silke. 'Oh, really. Do you expect us to trust *her* to tell us whether or not we should attack?' She shook her head gently at us both, as if she was a disappointed parent. 'She might be a clever girl, but her first loyalty obviously lies with you, not with her city.'

Silke cringed. But I didn't.

'That,' I said, with grim satisfaction, 'is why you're going to send your younger sister up to the clock tower with me instead.'

The king let out a bellow of outrage that shook the room. The crown princess's lips pressed tightly together ... but for the first time I saw real respect in her eyes.

The pride that Silke radiated as she looked at me was unmistakable.

But unlike Silke, I didn't smile, even when the commotion finally died down, the arguments ended and everyone eventually gave in.

Because now it was time to face my family.

CHAPTER 22

High at the top of the clock tower, a chill wind whipped through my hair and against my face, blowing over the waist-high stone walls and through the thin sleeves of my brown dress, and leaving goosebumps prickling all over my skin. The younger princess – Princess Sofia, the others had called her – wore a satin-lined hooded cloak that should have kept her warm against anything, but she still huddled in the far corner of the square tower, four feet away from me and scowling.

Scowling was good. If she'd looked afraid, I would have had to reassure her before my family could arrive. It wasn't safe to show fear in front of predators.

But I didn't have enough confidence to reassure anyone right now, least of all myself.

All I had was determination ... and my scale-cloth, as a tangible reminder. I held it close to my chest as I watched my family wing through the air, their forms looking more and more massive with every moment. They flew in a wide formation across the outer edge of the city, their great heads tilting to observe everything below. Now that I could finally make out their colours, I recognised Grandfather in the lead, Mother on his right, Aunt Tourmaline and Aunt Émeraude flying behind and ... was that actually Citrine, flying on his left? She hadn't been back for a visit in ages!

Whatever had brought them all here was clearly monumental, if they'd summoned Citrine away from her palace and her worshippers to take part.

And I was supposed to talk them out of it? All of the adults in my family together?

Even when I'd been a full dragon, they hadn't taken my opinions seriously. They'd all seen me as the restless, disobedient hatchling, the only one who couldn't settle into her education or find her passion, the one who kept on causing trouble for everyone. And now ...

As I watched them fly across the city, my breath shortened and my chest tightened until I was gasping with the memory of Grandfather's fireball flying towards me, warning me away from him and our family cave. At least on the mountainside I'd been able to roll away and escape. Here on the flat top of the clock tower, there was nowhere for me to go.

I looked down at the scale-cloth tucked against me. Then I took a deep breath, forcing the air through the rock-hard constriction in my chest, and loosened my grip on the cloth.

I would have recognised my family's scale patterns anywhere. Now I had to hope that they would recognise mine ... and be at least curious enough, after my weeks of absence, to investigate when they saw those familiar colours.

I shook out my scale-cloth and stood on tiptoes to hook one of its sleeves over the closest of the tall, pointed stone spikes that stood one at each corner of the clock tower. The wind whipped at the long cloth, trying to snatch it from my hands, but I knotted it on tightly and started for the next of the stone spikes, holding the free end of my scale-cloth in a tight grip.

Princess Sofia sneered at me. 'Do you really think building a shelter out of cloth will protect us from those beasts?'

'I'm not trying to protect us.' I stood as high on my tiptoes as I could, struggling to stretch the tip of one billowing trouser leg around the second stone spike. I had to tie it on carefully, or else the wind would blow it away within seconds. 'I'm trying to catch their attention.'

'Wonderful,' the princess muttered. 'Just wonderf– aaarrghhh!'

Her panic-filled yelp made me jerk around so fast I lost my grip on the scale-cloth. It shot out like a crimson-and-silver flag, streaming sideways in the wind between us, as the princess flattened herself into her corner, her eyes suddenly huge in her light brown face.

I didn't have time to investigate what had scared her. I jumped up, grabbing for the cloth – but it was too late. With a horrible tearing sound, it ripped free from the single stone spike where I had tied it and flew off into the air, whirling away from me across the city ...

... Directly towards the pack of dragons who had already shifted direction to fly straight for us, against the wind.

So *that* was what Sofia had yelped about.

As I watched, Mother tilted suddenly to the right, reaching out one massive forefoot to snag the tiny-looking scale-cloth on one claw before it could fly past her. When she caught it, she let out a roar of fury that shook the town hall beneath my feet and made my teeth and spine vibrate unbearably. Screams sounded from the streets and the building below us, but none of them slowed her down for an instant.

Tucking her forefeet and the trailing scale-cloth beneath her, she shot ahead of Grandfather, aiming straight for us like the point of a gigantic arrow, with the rest of my family forming the shape of a V behind her. I braced myself, clenching my hands into fists to keep myself steady.

'I think you got their attention.' The princess's voice shook.

'Don't act frightened,' I ordered, without looking back.

It was the only advice that I had time to give her.

As Mother hurtled towards us, her gigantic wings beat against the air, sending it buffeting against me until I had to grab the top of the closest stone wall with all my might to keep from being tossed over it.

'Tell me, human!' she roared. Her voice was like a great hammer beating against my head, making every bone in my body hurt. 'What have you creatures done with her?'

What?

I blinked at the raging creature before me, bigger than a house and puffing smoke from her giant nostrils. Was this really my mother, who'd always lectured me on staying calm and keeping in control? I had never seen her in such a fury. I hadn't even known that she was capable of it.

I stared at her, my mind whirling. '"Done with her"?' I repeated.

'Don't pretend ignorance now!' She slashed through the air with her right forefoot, trailing the scale-cloth behind her as she hovered just above the tower, her great wings flaring above her and her massive blue-and-gold face looming over me. Every one of her three-foot-long teeth was bared and gleaming in the sunlight. 'We know your people took her. We followed her scent, and you reek of it now, so you've been with her yourself. And now you're taunting us with *this*?' She slapped the scale-cloth against the tower. 'Did your human artists paint it while she lay trapped in one of your prisons? Was it a trophy of her capture, or worse? If you've hurt her, you'll pay with more than your lives!'

'Quick!' Princess Sofia hissed behind me. 'Give them the peace signal!'

But I had more important things to think about. Wonder blossomed in my chest as I stared into my mother's rage-filled golden eyes. 'Wait. You all came here looking ... for me?'

The next instant I had to dodge a giant smokeball as Mother snorted with fury. Cries of shock sounded from below, and I spared a moment to be grateful that the princess was up here with me, keeping any overexcited mages from letting loose their attacks.

But it was only a moment before Mother snarled, 'I'm not looking for you or for any other insignificant human. We're here to bring my daughter safely home!'

Well, then.

I straightened to my full height, letting go of the wall. I'd got the hang of bracing myself against the wind by then. And no matter how much I had been dreading it, I couldn't put this off any longer. I took a deep breath, looked into my mother's maddened gaze, and said:

'It's me, Mother. Aventurine. But I can't come home. See?' I held out my arms to show her. 'I was turned into a human.'

Mother jerked backwards so quickly I nearly fell over from the sudden gust of wind that hit me.

Then her mouth opened wider than I had ever seen it before, wide enough to swallow three of me. '*You dare lie to me now?*'

Suddenly all the other dragons were lunging forward to surround us, abandoning their formation to hone in on the clock tower, tails lashing, roaring as one in an overwhelming wave of sound that pummelled us from all directions.

'That's it!' Princess Sofia dived for the trapdoor. 'I'm telling them –'

'No!' I grabbed her cloak to pull her back. 'It's not too late. I just have to explain –'

'Humans always lie!' Grandfather snarled, and his hot breath swept across us, making Sofia let out a squeak of panic. 'I told you, daughter, you must be patient. It will take time to drag the truth from creatures who can't even understand honesty or sincerity.'

'*What?*' Sofia gave a jerk of outrage and stopped trying to get away. 'What did he just say about us?'

'Let me,' said Citrine smugly, and nudged Mother aside in mid-air. Her blue-and-silver scales shimmered in the sunlight as she lowered her massive head to watch us with a cold, assessing gaze. 'Allow me to explain the situation, puny humans. We have the ability to not only burn your city to the ground, but to create such a devastation across your countryside that it will never grow food for your species again. There will be stories told for a hundred years of the misfortunes of the kingdom that once existed here – before it made the mistake of incurring our wrath. Unless ...' She cocked her head to one side. 'All you need to do is release my foolish younger sister. If she is unharmed, we will be forgiving. But trust me,' she added sweetly, 'you do not wish to see my temper.'

The princess's eyes widened. 'She sounds just like my sister,' she whispered.

'I *know*.' I crossed my arms and glared up at my own big sister, who had always, *always* thought she could tell me what to do. And who exactly did she think she was calling *foolish*? 'Actually, Citrine, I'm not scared of you,' I yelled back. 'What are you really going to do – write an epic poem at us if we try to hold out against you? Because you know how much I hate your poetry! And no matter what you say, *no one* really needs to understand the stupid rules of iambic pentameter!'

The vertical pupils of Citrine's eyes snapped small and then large again. She hissed out a choking cloud of smoke. '*Aventurine?*'

'That is *not* Aventurine!' spat our mother. 'Look at her. She's human!'

Citrine's snout lowered towards us until it nearly touched my face. I didn't budge. I didn't lower my chin. I refused to even cough at the smoke that surrounded me. 'Well?' I demanded, my voice only slightly hoarse.

'She smells like Aventurine,' Citrine snarled. 'She's as stubborn and impertinent as Aventurine, too.'

Aunt Tourmaline nosed at me from my left. 'Is it normal for humans to have golden eyes?'

'No,' said Princess Sofia firmly. She was holding herself stiffly, with her arms wrapped tightly around her chest, but she looked too angry to be scared as she added, 'Trust me: nothing about this girl is *at all* normal.'

'And no one painted that cloth with my colours.' I pointed to the scale-cloth that still hung from Mother's claw. 'That's the only covering that was left on me after the spell of transformation.'

'*Spell?!*' Grandfather reared back, his scaly neck lengthening in his horror. 'I might have known! They tricked you and broke you. Didn't I tell you never to trust a human? My poor hatchling...'

'*Aventurine.*' And that was Mother, sounding more dangerous than I had ever heard her. Her voice was a hiss that slithered through the air, full of the promise of scorching violence and revenge. Her golden eyes fixed on me hypnotically, making every inch of me want to obey her. '*Tell me who did this to you.*'

I sighed heavily. 'A food mage,' I told her. 'But it's too late to make him pay. He's long gone. And besides –' I gritted my teeth, trying to hold the infuriating words back, but I couldn't stop myself from adding in a grim, unhappy mutter – 'he was only defending himself from being eaten.'

I hated the fact that nowadays I actually understood his point of view.

Mother lashed her tail, sending a nearby chimney toppling to the ground below. 'I *told* you not to leave the mountain. I told you!'

'Oh, Mother,' sighed Citrine, in her most aggravating tone. 'Aventurine never listened to anyone in her life. I always said that would lead to trouble, didn't I? And now she's been ruined and broken, all because you couldn't keep her in order. If you'd only –'

'Enough!' I roared, trembling with fury. 'Just listen to me, all of you, for once in your lives. *Listen!*' Panting, I glared at them, my fists clenched. 'I am *not* broken. And I am not ruined either! I've finally found my passion.'

'What?' All five of the dragons around me spoke at once, heat flaring over me.

Grandfather spoke over all the rest. 'What do you mean, you've found your passion? *Here?*' Smoke billowed out from his nostrils as he snorted with disbelief. 'You know humans don't understand true scholarship. Their tiny brains can't begin to comprehend the intellectual beauties of –'

'I *beg* your par–' the princess began indignantly.

But I spoke before she could finish. 'Humans have something better than scholarship,' I told them all. 'They have chocolate.'

Then I smiled a broad, human smile, as for once in my life I saw my whole family stunned into silence, all of them staring at me in incomprehension. For the first time ever, I understood something that even my older sister didn't.

'Just wait,' I said smugly. 'I'll show you all.'

CHAPTER 23

If Marina was surprised by her new customers, she didn't show it. She and Horst arrived less than an hour after Silke and three soldiers had been sent to fetch them from the Chocolate Heart. By then, the great square in front of the town hall had been cleared to make a space for my family to gather. The rest of the soldiers hadn't left, of course – they were waiting inside the town hall along with the frustrated battle mages, just in case something went wrong after all. The king and crown princess stood outside the front door, beside the lord mayor, wearing expressions that looked strained but gracious.

Princess Sofia wasn't standing with them. Instead she stood in the centre of the group of dragons, scowling and waving her arms energetically as she argued with my grandfather about the merits of human scholarship. Who could have guessed that a princess would be interested in dusty old philosophy books? I only wished that my brother was there to take part in the debate. Jasper would have absolutely loved it.

As Marina appeared at the furthest street corner, ahead of Horst and Silke, she took in the whole scene with one long look ... and then shrugged and marched on towards us, her face expressionless as ever.

Horst, Silke and the soldiers were all laden with covered hotplates and carrying heavy-looking packs on their backs that must have held even more. All that Marina carried was one enormous bundle in the shape of a giant presentation pot, wrapped up in towels to preserve the warmth.

I knew exactly what must be inside.

'Well, girl?' she said, as I ran over to greet her. Her gaze passed over the huge, magnificently scaled bodies of my family, all the way to the king, crown princess and lord mayor, who stood with frozen smiles on their faces. 'You were *this* determined to make me cook for royalty after all?'

'You came,' I said. A grin burst across my face, impossible to repress. 'You didn't freeze up this time, or have a moment.'

'Hmmph,' said Marina. 'I've had quite enough of those already. And besides ...' Her gaze rested on me, looking strangely enigmatic. 'You'd be surprised just how capable I felt of anything, after drinking a cup of your hot chocolate.'

Something in her words – and tone – made a tickling

sensation start up between my shoulders. *Something* ... But I didn't have time to ask for explanations. The king himself was beckoning to us.

'Our chocolatier has arrived!' He'd pitched his voice to carry through the square, and my relatives' massive heads swung around to follow as Marina walked steadily past them towards the king, with me at her side and Horst close behind. 'Madam Chocolatier, our, ah, honoured guests –' His Majesty gestured nervously towards my family – 'have requested a taste of your famous hot chocolate. They've heard that it's the best in the city, apparently.'

The lord mayor made an unintelligible sputtering noise. His face, I was pleased to see, was nearly purple with frustration.

'Of course! We are always delighted to provide for the king's most favoured guests.' Horst bowed sweepingly, first to the king, crown princess and lord mayor, and then to my family and Princess Sofia. His face might have looked significantly tighter than usual, and the whites of his eyes more noticeable, as his gaze took in the gigantic dragons who filled the square, but his businessman's smile never faltered. 'If we might set up our offerings?'

At a word from the king, two of the soldiers hurried inside to retrieve a long wooden table from the town hall. Then all three soldiers helped Horst and Silke empty out the sacks and hotplates, laying everything out in luxuriant profusion. Chocolate creams in tall, curving glasses stood beside chocolate tarts in silver pie dishes. Giant plates had been filled with larger-than-usual chocolate-almond conceits, next to even more new dishes I'd never seen before, which Marina must have invented while I was away. The unmistakable heavenly smell of chocolate rose from the table to twine through the crisp autumn air, and every dragon head lifted to breathe it in.

Ten golden eyes gleamed in reaction. Five golden gazes fixed with intense interest upon the table.

Marina stepped forward at the last, pulling off the thick towels that had protected a two-foot-high presentation pot in shining silver. She set the massive pot in the centre of the table, smirking at Horst. 'You see?' she said. 'Not so stupid of me after all to cart this thing all the way from Villenne!' Then she turned to me, dusting off her hands. 'Aventurine? Would you care to do the honours this time?'

Oh, would I!

Using all of the muscles that I'd built up in her kitchen, I raised the giant, heavy pot in both hands and slowly, carefully tipped it to pour the dark, steaming chocolate into the five empty bowls that waited nearby.

Hissing sounded from all around the square as the smell of hot chocolate floated through the air. I inhaled deeply as I poured, recognising every scent inside it: vanilla, nutmeg, and, oh yes ...

'I thought they might like plenty of chilli in their chocolate,' said Marina, 'just like you do.'

I gave the first bowl to Grandfather, of course. But I carried Mother her bowl next, and I kept my eyes on hers as I set the bowl on the ground in front of her, my chest tightening. 'Just taste it,' I told her. 'You'll understand.'

Please understand, I added silently. I wouldn't demean myself by saying it out loud. But I couldn't move away from her either. I just stood there, waiting, leaving the rest of my family unserved.

Mother looked down at me for a long moment. I curled my fingers tightly into my palms as I recognised that look. It was the same look she'd given me a hundred times before, as she'd prepared to find out exactly how far behind I was in all of my studies.

It was a look that said she hoped to be surprised ... but didn't expect it.

Then she lowered her massive snout and daintily, carefully, stretched her long, forked tongue towards the bowl.

No one in the square said a word as her tongue flicked out again and again ... and again. Then the bowl was suddenly empty, and her golden eyes flared wide as she looked back at me with an expression I had never seen on her face before. 'You can make *this*?' she demanded.

'She can,' said Marina, from just behind me. I hadn't even heard her join me, I'd been so focused on my mother. Marina's voice was steady and calm, though, and her hand landed firmly on my shoulder, grounding me. 'She's the best apprentice I've ever had.'

'*Aventurine*?' said Citrine. 'But – !'

Her voice cut off as Mother's tail flicked warningly, sending a gust of wind rushing across the square.

'Quiet!' Mother told my older sister, for the first time that I could remember. 'Taste your chocolate.'

Citrine's eyes narrowed. But when I brought over her

bowl of hot chocolate, she drank it all without a single word.

It was one of the most delicious moments of my life. And when I looked across at the younger princess, I could see from her smile that she understood it completely.

It didn't take long for my family to devour the entire tableful of chocolate treats that Marina had brought from the Chocolate Heart. Silke made certain that the royals had some, too, serving all of them with a flourish. The king ate his chocolate tart with obvious appreciation, the crown princess's eyebrows rose higher and higher as she ate three chocolate-almond conceits in a row and I saw something very near bliss on Princess Sofia's face as she slowly drank her cup of hot chocolate, visibly savouring every sip.

The lord mayor, of course, claimed that he wasn't hungry, until a meaningful look from the king changed his mind. But the sulky expression on his face at the end, as he used his spoon to scrape up every last, nearly invisible speck of chocolate cream from his glass, was even more satisfying than any applause could have been.

When Grandfather had emptied his very last bowl, he let out a sigh that billowed warmth across the square and made my brown dress flutter. 'Well.' He looked down at me indulgently, with a thin line of smoke dribbling happily from his snout. 'It seems to me, hatchling, that you haven't done so badly for yourself after all.'

Aunt Émeraude said, 'It will certainly be useful to have someone in the family who can make *that* for us!'

'Oh yes,' said Aunt Tourmaline. '*Deliciously* useful.'

'But I'm not going back with you,' I told them. 'You do understand that, don't you?'

Grandfather's eyes narrowed. His snout lowered. 'You may have lost your proper shape, due to typical human trickery –' his voice deepened into a snarl, and out of the corner of my eye, I saw the king flinch – 'but you are still our own hatchling, to be guarded and cherished. Do you expect us to leave you here, unprotected, among strangers?'

'It's my territory now,' I said. 'And they're not strangers to me. They're not even all that different from dragons. Not really.'

The king coughed pointedly, stepping forward. 'Er ... as happy as we are that you've found comfort in our city, young lady, we wouldn't like ... that is, if your family truly desires –'

'No,' Mother said abruptly. 'She shouldn't come back.'

This time, I was the one who flinched. It was only for a moment, of course. Then I lifted my chin and put on my fiercest expression, shoving down the pain and reminding myself that this was exactly what I'd wanted. 'That's fine,' I said stiffly. 'I know I never did what you wanted.'

'Child ...' Mother stretched her long, gleaming, blue-and-golden neck across the square until her great golden eyes were looking directly down at me. 'Haven't you ever listened to a word I've said? I always wanted you to find your passion. Now that that has finally happened, why would I be cruel enough to pull you away from it?'

Oh. Suddenly, my throat felt choked with something that I couldn't understand.

'You're not angry?' I said, my voice small. 'Or disappointed in me? Again?'

She shook her massive head, but her gaze never wavered from my face. 'I have rarely felt so proud of anyone in my life.'

That was it. My throat closed up entirely.

Marina spoke from behind me, looking straight into my mother's gaze as I forced back the sudden moisture from my own eyes. 'Don't worry,' Marina said. 'We'll take care of her.'

'Did you really think we'd leave her without any protection?' Grandfather snorted, a low growl rumbling through his throat. 'If our hatchling *is* to be left in this city after all, we'll be keeping a very close eye on it from now on.'

'You will?' The king's voice came out as a near squeak, his face paling.

'Absolutely.' Grandfather's tail lashed dangerously. 'If any enemy army ever thinks of attacking, they'll change their minds before they come within fifty miles of our hatchling, I can promise you that!'

'Oh. Oh!' The king blinked rapidly. 'Well, in that case –' his lips stretched into a wide, beaming smile – 'we would be more than happy to enter into an alliance with your family!'

'Indeed.' The crown princess smiled coolly as she looked across my family's massive armoured bodies. 'And I think we can safely promise you that your, ah, *hatchling* will be well cared for in her new home, under our own royal protection.'

'Ahem ...' Silke cleared her throat delicately. 'Unless the Chocolate Heart goes out of business, you mean, because of persecution and rumours, so Marina and Horst and Aventurine all have to flee the city?'

Every dragon head in the square swung around to stare at her. Snarls tore through the air.

'What are you talking about?' Grandfather demanded. '*Out of business?* Persecution? Rumours?'

'No!' The king started forward, waving his arms desperately. 'Ahaha. No, no, no. There's nothing at all to worry about, my very dear ... friends. After all, why on earth would the Chocolate Heart go out of business when it famously makes the best hot chocolate in the city? There may have been a few mistakes made in the past, but –' he puffed out his chest – 'from now on it will have my *personal* patronage, and there is no other chocolate house that can boast of that! In fact, I believe the Chocolate Heart will soon be the most successful chocolate house in this city, as well as the best!'

'Mmmph!' The lord mayor let out a muffled groan.

The crown princess turned to give him a long look. 'Isn't that right, My Lord Mayor?' she asked gently. 'Don't you want to reassure our new allies too?'

His shoulders sagged. His chest rose and fell. Even his big floppy hat seemed to sigh. But finally he gave us all a sickly-looking smile. 'Of course,' he said. 'The Chocolate Heart will have all of our wholehearted support.'

'*Excellent,*' hissed Mother. 'And we'll see that for ourselves, of course, as we'll be making regular visits from now on.'

At that the king began to tug at his neck-knot, looking more than a little green. But a canny gleam lit up the crown princess's eyes as she stepped forward and began to talk smoothly about trade agreements and safe passageways. Soon she and Citrine were involved in a long and exquisitely courteous debate, while my mother and grandfather listened with sharp attention and my aunts whispered together in a language of their own that no one else had ever managed to understand ...

And I was left standing at the sidelines with Silke and Marina, watching it all with deep satisfaction.

'I know exactly what my next handbill is going to say.' Silke held out her hands as if to frame it. '"The chocolate shop that saved the city! Chocolate so good, it melted even a dragon's heart!"'

Marina rolled her eyes. 'More nonsense,' she muttered. But then she smiled at both of us indulgently. 'I hope you're almost ready to go home,' she said, 'because apparently, we have a lot of work to do.'

When we walked back into the kitchen of the Chocolate Heart an hour later, the first thing I saw was the presentation pot of hot chocolate that I had used earlier that day, still sitting on the counter. I scooped it up, starting for the sink.

'Hold on.' Marina spoke from behind me. 'Aren't you going to taste it first? There's still a full cup's worth left at least.'

'But it'll be cold by now.' I frowned. 'How can I learn anything from that?'

'Actually –' Marina studied me, her expression enigmatic – 'I think we might all learn quite a lot. You see, I've been thinking.' She nodded at Silke. 'You remember what this one was jabbering on about earlier?'

'I beg your pardon!' said Silke, throwing herself down on a chair. 'I've never jabbered in my life! I often talk at length, of course, but it's always interesting, and –'

'About Aventurine's hot chocolate,' Marina interrupted. 'How it made you want this place to succeed, when you'd been ready to abandon it before.'

'Oh. That.' Silke shrugged and tucked her hands into her pockets. 'Well, that part's absolutely true.'

'Hmm.' Marina turned back to me. 'Well, I didn't feel any different after I drank that first hot chocolate – but then, I wanted to save this place already. Horst went wild over the taste of your tarts, though, even though they were so burned they should have tasted like ash. Looking back, I think I probably should have tried them, too. Because ...'

She gestured towards the chocolate pot. 'I drank a cup of that hot chocolate today,' she said, 'and I can tell you, I was feeling heartily discouraged before I began to drink. There was a whole bunch of dragons getting ready to burn down the city ... we were losing this chocolate house, no matter what ... and worst of all, I'd had to use a substandard recipe for a chocolate custard, just to make this fellow happy.' She jerked her shoulder towards the doorway where Horst stood.

'Ahem!' said Horst, shaking his head at her. 'It was not a substandard recipe. I liked it!'

'As I said.' Marina crossed her arms. 'But then I drank that hot chocolate. And within the first two sips, I was feeling more confident than I ever have before in my life – and believe me, that is saying something. All of a sudden, I *knew* I could do anything I put my mind to. Even cooking for the king, when the summons came. I didn't feel a single moment of nerves.'

A shiver brushed down the top of my spine. 'What are you trying to say?'

'What I'm saying,' she said steadily, 'is that I'd be very interested to hear what exactly you were thinking about when you made that particular pot of hot chocolate.'

'I ...' I shook my head, feeling dazed, as I tried to remember. It all seemed to have happened a very long time ago. 'I think I was deciding ... that I could be whatever I wanted to be. A dragon *and* a girl. Both of them, together.'

'Mm-hmm.' Marina nodded. 'I thought it might have been something like that.' She scooped a porcelain cup off from the rows of hooks on the closest wall and held it out to me. 'Here,' she told me. 'Pour yourself a cup. But I think you'd better drink it outside, just in case.'

There was a distant buzzing noise in my head as I accepted the cup from her.

Vaguely, I was aware of Silke talking excitedly nearby as I poured myself the hot chocolate, but I couldn't take in anything that she said. I couldn't even think. I didn't want to. I was afraid to let my mind take in Marina's words. Afraid to believe ...

Holding my mind as still and frozen as a block of ice, I

walked through the swinging doors into the main room, balancing the full cup of liquid steady in my hand. I pushed open the front door of the Chocolate Heart and stepped outside into the chilly late-afternoon air. For once our busy street was empty. Maybe everyone was still hiding under a bridge or inside their houses, waiting to find out if they were safe.

I was glad that no one else was here to see me.

But I didn't let myself think about why that might be as I lifted the cup to my lips and took my first sip of the cool, sweet, spicy chocolate. Then I gulped the rest down in one long rush.

A burst of flame filled my mouth as the chilli exploded against my senses.

My eyes closed. A wave of warm, pure certainty flooded through me. My mouth fell open in amazement.

This was right. This was me. How could I ever have doubted it?

And: *Was this really waiting inside me all along?*

I tilted my head back and roared with joy as my wings exploded from my sides, wide and strong and perfect as ever. Claws shot out from my hands as I erupted outwards, suddenly just as big on the outside as I'd always felt inside.

Warmth surrounded me. Power filled me.

I flexed my long, sharp claws and opened my eyes to look down on my second family. Horst was staring, open-mouthed, through the glass of the chocolate-house window. Silke stood outside beside me, bouncing on her heels and laughing with delight.

'Aventurine!' she yelled. 'You're massive!'

Standing in the open doorway of the Chocolate Heart, Marina gave me a small satisfied smile and a nod. 'Well?' she said. 'And how about the rest? A dragon *and* a girl, both at once, remember?'

Oh. I'd almost forgotten. But there it was, clear and bright within me. I closed my eyes, focused ...

And there they were again, when I looked: my small and clever human fingers.

I would never manage any proper cooking with dragon claws, after all.

Silke grabbed my hand, whooping with delight. Two weeks ago, I would have pulled away; now I wrapped my human fingers around hers to hold on tight. Joy filled me as I looked up at Marina and thought of my mother, who was already planning her next visit to the city.

I might have a new home, but I hadn't lost my first one after all ... because that food mage had passed on more to me than he'd ever intended in that first, panic-filled moment of transformation. Now my wings were waiting for me whenever I wanted them.

It was almost too much happiness to contain. But I was a dragon and a girl, and I was strong enough for all of it.

Horst shook his head and smiled as he stepped outside to join us. Wrapping one arm around Marina's shoulders, he raised his free hand to point at all the windows that had been flung open up and down the street, and at all the neighbours who were staring out at us in silent shock.

'Somehow,' he told us, 'I'm guessing this is going to be a very interesting week for our chocolate house. And I think it may finally be time to hire more staff.'

CHAPTER 24

'This is so unfair,' Jasper told me six weeks later. It wasn't the first time he'd said it, and I knew it wouldn't be the last.

It made me tingle with wicked delight every time.

He sighed as he licked the last of the hot chocolate from around his snout, shifting in his cushion of gold coins and sending them skittering across the cavern floor. 'You were never even interested in humans, unlike me!' he pointed out. 'And now you get to *be* one, whenever you want. But Mother won't even let me visit you there! She says she's still not sure it's safe.'

'It's safe,' I told him. 'You can trust me on that. Those royals are determined not to displease us, now that they have a dragon guard for their capital city. Every other kingdom is jealous of them – and apparently it's wonderful for trade.'

'Hmmph.' Moodily, Jasper scraped at the mound of gold coins with his claw. 'That Princess Sofia of yours has some interesting theories on the differences between draconic and human scholarship. It would be nice to get to talk them over in person instead of having to stick to letters all the time.'

'I could always turn you human for a day or two, if you wanted,' I offered. 'I'm getting better at that sort of thing.'

I hardly even flinched any more when I remembered that I was a terrifying food mage. It helped that Marina genuinely didn't care, just as long as I didn't let my new-found powers make me lazy in her kitchen.

And *that* was never going to happen. I knew what I could do nowadays, and it only made me work harder than ever to control myself. I would never change anyone else against their will, the way that I'd been changed all those weeks ago.

Silke insisted that she didn't mind having been my first victim. After all, deciding to support the chocolate house had brought her more chocolate in the last seven weeks than most people ate in their entire lifetimes. Also, she'd negotiated herself a fabulous salary as Horst's new assistant ... although she'd insisted that it be a part-time role. She could never stay in just one place for a whole day. But she was a brilliant waitress for the chocolate house whenever she chose to be there, and her handbills brought in more and more new customers every day.

So, no, I didn't feel guilty about what I'd done to my first real friend ... but I had learned to be very careful.

Still ... my brother didn't need to know that, did he? Tongue in cheek, I grinned at him, making my voice sickly sweet. 'I *probably* wouldn't accidentally turn you into a slug,' I told him, 'just by thinking the wrong thing as I was making your hot chocolate. Although if I did –' carefully, discreetly, I shifted to one side, bracing every muscle for action but innocently holding his gaze all the while – 'would it really make all that much of a difference?'

'Arrrrgh!' Smoke flying from his mouth, Jasper leaped for me.

But I was already moving.

Just as I'd planned, my brother landed on the prickly mountain of diamonds, emeralds and other gemstones that rose just behind the spot where I'd been sitting a moment earlier. He came out sneezing, shaking his head and roaring louder than ever, and he pounced on my back as I fled, snorting smokeballs.

Soon we were rolling around and around on the floor, sending tiaras and precious stones flying into the air.

'Children!' Mother sighed heavily as she crawled into the cavern, squeezing her glittering bulk through the main entryway. 'Can't I ever trust the two of you to behave together?' Shaking her head, she dropped what she'd been holding. 'Here. We brought back food from the hunt for you both.'

Abandoning Jasper, I pounced on the feast. He grabbed

the other end of it, and we grinned at each other in perfect accord over our delicious meaty meal.

It wasn't human, of course. My family had a new rule about that. Humans were not *always* to be avoided – not any more – but they were never, ever to be eaten.

Dragons always protected their families.

An hour later, it was time to go. I hooked the handle of my empty hot-chocolate pot over one claw and hung the sack that had held my family's other chocolatey treats over another.

'Be good,' Mother told me as I left the cave. She gave me one of her sternest looks. 'Make us proud, and remember: you're coming back here on your very next afternoon off!'

'I will,' I promised. 'I always do.'

And as I was climbing up the long tunnel that led out of the mountain, Jasper yelled after me, 'Don't forget to give my letter to the princess!'

Grandfather was still shaking his head over that as I emerged into the open air, to the spot where he'd been waiting for me. 'Oh, my hatchlings. What you've both come to ...'

But he held out one massive forefoot, just like always, and I curled myself happily against his warm, scaly chest as both of his forelegs closed around me, holding me safe behind his giant claws.

A moment later, his great wings were beating against the air. We flew up together into the cold, clear sky in the early twilight, soaring high above the mountainside towards Drachenburg.

In a few years – well, possibly as many as thirty years, if Mother really did have her way – I'd finally be able to fly myself back and forth from our mountain to the city. Perhaps I ought to have been furious about how long I would have to wait. In the old days, after all, it had driven me wild not to be allowed to rely on my own wings yet. But just now, after everything that I'd been through ...

The truth was, it felt absolutely fine to look down at the trees and the mountainside below from the shelter of my grandfather's big claws, with his strong wings sweeping out around us as darkness crept across the sky. In fact, as I looked down on that rocky mountainside where my life had changed forever, I had to admit: if I ever saw that rascally food mage again ...

Well, I certainly wouldn't thank him. I was a dragon, not a worm! But I wouldn't flame him either ... because I wouldn't change what I had now for the world.

Soon, of course, Grandfather would be leaving me again, in the city square closest to the Chocolate Heart, which was always cleared in preparation for his arrival. But even after he flew away, I wouldn't mind being apart from my family any more. After all, I knew I'd be back on my next afternoon off, in only seven days. And in the mean-time ...

Mmm. When I closed my eyes, I could already imagine what would be waiting for me in the kitchen of the Chocolate Heart when I walked back inside in my human form tonight.

The smell of roasting cocoa beans would fill the air,

and Marina would be standing by the stove, ready to teach me a new recipe.

Resting in my grandfather's claws, I breathed a happy line of smoke from my nose and dreamed of chocolate all the way home.

ACKNOWLEDGEMENTS

ACKNOWLEDGEMENTS

Thank you so much to my older son for asking me to tell him the story of The Dragon with a Chocolate Heart as I wrote it, for drawing dozens of fabulous alternative book covers along the way and for talking so enthusiastically about the story with me as we sat eating chocolate cakes in our favourite cafe. I love sharing my stories with you! And I can't wait for you to share your own stories with the world.

Thank you to both of my sons for sharing and expanding my love of dragons and for helping me to wrestle with our obstreperous printer until it finally spat out working copies for my edits. You guys made me laugh and have fun with the process ... and my edits got done in time after all. Whew!

Thank you so much to everyone who beta-read raw, first-draft chapters of *The Dragon with a Chocolate Heart* and cheered me on: Patrick Samphire, Jenn Reese, Deva Fagan, Rene Sears and Beth Bernobich. I can't even tell you guys just how much your support meant to me! And I'm so grateful to everyone who critiqued all or part of the finished manuscript: Ying Lee, Patrick Samphire, Deva Fagan, R.J. Anderson, Susie Day, David Burgis, Laura Florand, Jenn Reese and Tricia Sullivan. I appreciate your help so much!

I owe a huge debt of thanks to my fabulous agent, Molly Ker Hawn, for believing in my book and in me, for giving me such great edits pre-submission and for selling this book so beautifully. Thank you, Molly! There isn't enough chocolate in the world to show all of my appreciation.

Thank you so much to my wonderful editors, Ellen Holgate and Sarah Shumway, for giving Aventurine a perfect home at Bloomsbury, and for helping me to tell her story as well as possible. I'm so grateful for the smart, thoughtful and thorough edits and for the great brainstorming help. And thank you so much to Vicky Leech for your fabulous organisational skills (and great taste in chocolate, too)!

I owe a big thanks to Talya Baker for careful copy-editing of the manuscript, and to Helen Vick for managing the editorial process *and* sharing wonderful musical recommendations.

Thank you so much to the Royal Literary Foundation, without whose generous support I would never have been able to write this book in the first place.

And, as always, thank you so much to my husband, Patrick Samphire, for supporting me every step of the way – and for making me the best hot chocolates, always. I'm so lucky to be married to you!

$1 \times 3 = 3$

$2 \times 3 = 6$

$3 \times 3 = 9$

$4 \times 3 = 12$

$5 \times 3 = 15$

$6 \times$